Kingdom Level Six

Kingdom, Volume 6

Adam Drake

Published by Adam Drake, 2024.

Kingdom Level Six
(Kingdom Series Book 6)
By
Adam Drake
Copyright © 2024

KINGDOM LEVEL SIX

First edition. June 30, 2024.

ISBN: 979-8227263551

Written by Adam Drake.

Also by Adam Drake

An Infinite Cats Mystery
The Big Bag of Infinite Cats: A Cozy Mystery
Magical Mischief: A Cozy Mystery
The River's Dream: A Cozy Mystery
The Model Prisoner

Bitch Berserker
Bitch Berserker: LitRPG Dark Fantasy

Fantasy Double Series
Fantasy Double Series 1

Fantasy & Scifi Double Series
Fantasy & Scifi Double Series 1

Fringe Outlaws
Escape to the Fringe

Kingdom
Kingdom Level One: LitRPG Epic Fantasy
Kingdom Level Two: LitRPG Epic Fantasy
Kingdom Level Three: LitRPG Epic Fantasy
Kingdom Level Four: LitRPG Epic Fantasy
Kingdom Level Five
Kingdom Level Six
Kingdom Level Seven

Kingdom Bundles
Kingdom LitRPG Bundle: Books 1-4
Kingdom LitRPG Bundle: Books 5-7

LitRPG Double Series
LitRPG Double Series 1: Epic Adventure Fantasy
LitRPG Double Series 2: Epic Adventure Fantasy
LitRPG Double Series 3: Epic Adventure Fantasy
LitRPG Double Series 4: Epic Adventure Fantasy

LitRPG: Shadow For Hire
Shadow Gambit: LitRPG Adventure Fantasy
Shadow Hunting: LitRPG Adventure Fantasy
Shadow Wars: LitRPG Adventure Fantasy
Shadow Blade: LitRPG Adventure Fantasy

Mage Level Grind
Mage Level 1
Mage Level 2
Mage Level 3
Mage Level 4
Mage Level 5

SCIFI Double Series
SCIFI Double Series 1: Action Adventure

Total Collapse: Day By Day
The First Day: Post Apocalyptic Thriller

Standalone
Shadow For Hire Books 1-4: LitRPG Adventure Fantasy
The LitRPG Super Bundle: Epic Adventure Fantasy
LitRPG: 5 Books: Epic Adventure Fantasy
SCIFI Double Novel: Science Fiction Adventure
Fantasy Collection: 6 Novels
Science Fiction Collection: 6 Novels
Scifi & Fantasy Megabundle: 12 Novels
Infinite Cats Mysteries: Books 1-3
Mage Levels 1-5

KINGDOM LEVEL SIX

A dungeon to delve into.

With the revelation of a potential way to escape from this world, Robert must explore his very first dungeon in the search for its clues.

But the Dead City is not a place for the meek, and he must tread carefully. There are dangers hidden in its quiet streets, which he must be wary of.

And he still has a kingdom to run, with projects to approve and the beginnings of an army to train.

The job of an adventurer king is never done.

CHAPTER ONE

"We're going to be rich!" Erwin cried.

The dock master clapped his hands and danced a jig as a boat full of fish was pulled up onto the beach.

"That's a good haul," Robert said, peering into the boat. It was packed full of squirming, twitching fish of all kinds and varieties.

"Every haul is a good haul, my lord," Erwin said. "Considering how long we couldn't even fish. But, thanks to you, we can now fish all day!"

It had been nearly a week since Rob and Fenton had pulled out the sarcophagus from its watery grave. The fish had returned, and Erwin had organized a small army of fishermen to reap the ocean of its new bounty.

Rob looked out to the horizon. Two other boats were casting their nets, having unloaded their previous hauls. The boats had been made by one of Gunther's apprentices, while the carpenter was busy with the town wall. The nets had been provided by Zuthus, who was giddy at the prospect of trading for fish, a troglodyte staple.

But Rob was more focused on the distant horizon, scanning for a sail, a harbinger of the shadow pirates lurking in the deeper waters. He was worried they would attack his fishermen, and rightly so. Although they had not made an appearance, he knew they were still out there.

Yet, Erwin insisted that as long as the boats stayed within sight of shore, the pirates wouldn't be a problem. And so far, it was true. The fishing went on without a hitch, with the carpenter apprentice finishing a carved boat every couple of days, adding to the kingdom's tiny flotilla.

Rob watched as Erwin barked orders at the people on the beach. Some filled large baskets provided by the Troglodytes and hauled them up the cliffside path. An array of baskets had been placed at the top, awaiting pickup by the trogs. Others hauled fish up the path to another area. Here, between the beach and the grassy fields, had been assembled dozens of dry racks made of branches. Fish were hung on them to dry in the warm morning sun. Once finished, they will be taken back to town to be enjoyed by the people, while a portion would be given to Zuthus, who had clients to sell them to.

Saif appeared at the top of the cliffside path, and waved, robe billowing comically with the ocean breeze.

Rob grabbed four baskets, two to a hand, and carried them up with relative ease. People glanced at him wide eyed, and chuckled. He had discovered putting points in his Strength attribute made him stronger than most others and he marveled at what he could carry. He never could do this in real life, only in a video game.

He dropped off his haul and turned to the Sage, who was counting the baskets. "How much for all these?"

Saif did some quick math in his head. "Maybe one hundred to one hundred and twenty gold."

Rob's eyes lit up. "That much? Just for this?" He hadn't expected the price of fish to be so valuable.

"It's a good haul, my lord. The different species off our coast are in high demand, especially with the trogs. If we keep expanding the fishing fleet, and stocks can be maintained, I expect we could easily make one thousand gold per day, after costs, of course."

Rob marveled. Maybe he should hang up his sword and become a fisherman. "It looks like Erwin has a good handle on the situation. He can manage things until we can get around to building a proper dock." The dock they had was old and dilapidated. And it wasn't suitable for larger ships to use, according to Erwin.

Saif said, "Before a dock can be built there is the small matter of the pirates. No one can even attempt to approach our shore while they skulk out there."

Rob sighed. "It's on my to-do list, don't worry. But, for now, let's just enjoy what we have." The truth was he had no idea how to deal with the shadow pirates. They were ethereal beings, and could control water, as he had seen them do. He was hoping something would come up which would help him. He knew the game would provide him with the means, eventually.

A town guard called out, and pointed west. "Trogs, my lord!"

Several reptilian humanoids emerged from the forest and waded across the shallow creek. It was the largest group of their kind he had seen since he first encountered them. For a moment, he was a little alarmed at their number, but noticed only four were actually armed, carrying the long tridents they favored. Amongst them was the only human, a woman. Ynette.

As the trogs approached en masse, Rob noticed the handful of his guards clutching their weapons nervously. He waved at them to calm down.

"Lord Barron, First Sage Saif. Hail, and well met," Ynette said. All the trogs stood back, casting hungry eyes at all the baskets of fish.

"Hail, and well met," Rob returned. He didn't know when the phrase had started to be used, but he liked it. "I see you've brought help."

She smiled. "The Crimson Council is eager to indulge in fresh fish. It has been a long time for them." She looked over the baskets, then down at the boats just off the shore. "Can we expect such an amount each day?"

Saif said, "This, and possibly more, once we put more boats to sea. Will that be to your liking?"

"Definitely. The council's hunger for this staple is practically bottomless," she chuckled.

Rob said, "Well, as long as their coin bag is just as bottomless, we will be happy to provide for them."

All three humans laughed, while the trogs watched.

Ynette paid Saif, then motioned to the others. The trogs picked up the baskets and headed back to their caves.

"Did you speak to the council about what we talked about before?" Rob said. Ever since the mercenary leader, Peter, had mentioned the potential of raiders attacking from the east, Rob had become paranoid of an invasion. But not only from the east, but from the west, as well. He knew nothing threatening would be allowed to through the Trog Pass in the southeast, but he was more worried about what could come over the western mountains.

"They give their reassurance that no one can gain access to your kingdom via the tunnels. Certainly it may be possible for an individual to get through, and especially if aided by magic. But, as for a large force, it wouldn't be allowed."

Rob said, "What about over the mountains?"

She frowned a little. "That cannot be guaranteed, unfortunately. The mountains are vast, and the trogs usually avoid the cold. It has a more drastic effect on their bodies than other beings. But we do keep watch where we can. If a force were to attempt to cross over the mountains, we will give you a warning."

That really didn't do much at putting Rob's mind at ease, but there was only so much which could be done, by either himself, or the trogs.

He also knew he couldn't really count on the trogs in the event of an invasion. Ynette had been apologetic, but emphatic that the trogs didn't involve themselves in 'above ground' disputes. So Rob didn't press her further on the matter.

"I appreciate you talking to them for me," Rob said.

With that, she left, flanked by her guards.

Rob watched them cross the creek and vanish into the forest. "I want to put a guard up at their tunnel entrance."

Saif blinked. "Do you not trust them, my lord?"

The words of the man who spoke through Greta was still fresh in his mind. "At this point, I can't afford to trust anyone. But having any armed group, trogs or otherwise, wandering around my kingdom doesn't sit well with me."

"What will you do about the mountain passes? You cannot guard all of them."

Rob said, "I have an idea I want to run past Fenton. We may not be able to guard all the mountain ranges, but we can, at least, mitigate the risk."

A man ran over to them, calling and waving. Rob recognized him as one of Gunther's workers.

"My lord! Gunther needs you, right away!" he said.

"Why? Is something wrong?" Rob said, instinctively grabbing at his sword.

"It's the wall, my lord! He has found something!"

CHAPTER TWO

They walked briskly back to Hope with Rob far in the lead. But after only a few minutes, he summoned his horse, Henry, and rode the rest of the way.

As he approached his kingdom's meager little capital, he was struck at how much progress had been made on the wall. Nearly half the town was now encircled by a tall wall of logs, each firmly placed together and embedded several feet into the ground. The entire south side was more or less complete, and much of the east side was done. The entry points, where gates would be erected, were at the south and east. On the west side, pressed up against the castle hill, was a smaller entrance which Gunther referred to as a future sally port. It was meant to allow attacks on enemies during sieges, something Rob hoped would never needed to be used.

Rob found Gunther and Trenton near the eastern entrance. A small group of workers were gathered around something in the trench they were digging for the wall.

Dismounting, Rob approached and looked down into the dugout. "What did you find?"

Gunther pointed. "Something I thought you should see, my lord."

At the bottom of the trench, partially covered by muddy water was what appeared to be a large box. Whatever it was, it looked out of place. Treasure?

Ensuring all his buffs were active, Rob dropped down into the trench for a closer look. After a moment's hesitation, he put a hand on it.

Nothing happened. No message indicating what it was, nor was there a magical explosion. At least it wasn't trapped.

There were strange, squiggly markings across its entire surface, but he couldn't recognize if it was even writing. The object resembled a trunk, rectangular in shape, and with a seam around one side.

Rob tried to shift it, but after a lot of grunting, had to give up. It appeared to be made of stone. What was it?

Unger, the shard scholar, pushed his way through the gathered workers and peered down. After a moment of inspection, the man gasped.

"Do you know what it is?" Rob said, alarmed by the man's reaction.

"Yes, I do, my lord!" He quickly climbed down the embankment, but slipped and fell into the mud.

Workers laughed, but went instantly silent when Rob arched a brow in their direction.

Unger barely noticed his muddy clothes, so entranced by the object. "This looks like a Relic Box. And look, there are the three keyholes. It is! By the Many-Hells, I never thought I would live to see the day where I would be in the presence of one!"

Rob said, "Could you expand on that a little?"

"Relic Boxes were used by the Gods of old to store their valuable items. It is said each box had the ability to contain items of powerful magic. Each was sealed with three keys. Find those keys, and you can unlock this box."

Rob peered at the box, and made out three faded keyholes, more like minor indentations than something to insert a key. "Is it dangerous? Can we move it?"

"I believe so. What danger it might have would be within."

Rob sighed. He certainly didn't have any keys to try and he seriously doubted he would be of a high enough level to use what was inside. Regardless of the thing's potential value, he needed it out if the way so work could continue. "Trenton, would you mind taking this to the storage house for now?"

"Not a problem," the builder said and climbed down. But when he used his levitation on it, the box barely moved, only wiggled in the mud.

"Wow," Trenton said. "Something is incredibly heavy inside."

He bellowed for his son, Benton, to come help, and they worked on moving the box. It took everything they had, between the two of them, just to levitate it out of the trench.

Rob guided them to one of the houses the town used to store supplies. He had them place it under the stairwell, then covered it with a blanket.

Relic box, huh? He wondered what kind of nonsense was inside and whether it was designed to help or hinder his chances of escaping this place. He thanked the builders and let them return to their respective tasks.

He was walking to the house Fenton used as the main headquarters for the town guard, when Greta appeared from a side street. Carrying a basket of thrush-berries, she waved and continued in her way.

Seeing her gave Rob a chill. Having witnessed her used as a vessel, by someone outside this world to speak to him, had been unnerving. And the fact she had no memory of it happening added to the creepiness of the encounter.

Rob had gotten little sleep since then, with his mind reeling at the implications. He had an ally on the outside, someone who was trying to help him escape. Or so they claimed. Still, just the thought of someone, *anyone*, giving a damn about his situation made him feel a little less lost. Until now, he had no one to communicate with about what was really going on. But having a brief exchange with that someone meant a lot to his overall mental state. He wasn't going insane. This was a simulation, and an individual involved with it wanted to help.

Rob found Fenton in his headquarters handing a sword to a new recruit, a young woman, who stood at attention.

When the two saw their king, they both froze in surprise.

Rob waved a hand. "Please, don't let me interrupt."

Fenton nodded then turned back to the recruit, who was now sweating. "You will be assigned to the Crossroads rotation. Seek out the village captain, and he will fill you in on your duties."

He dismissed her, and she gave him a nod. As she passed Rob, she bowed. "My lord," she said, before hurrying out the door.

"How is the Crossroads deployment going?" Rob asked.

"Stretched thin, I'm afraid to say, my lord," Fenton said. He pulled out a parchment from a desk which listed the names of all the members of the Town Guard. "With the reinforcing of the south and east passes, we have very few people left for other duties. I've even had to strip down the Hope detachment to the bare minimum. Per your suggestion, I've removed the guards from the mine and quarry, but even that barely covers the night rotations. We need more people, my lord."

Ever since Rob had demanded the wall be built at top speed, all other areas of the kingdom were suffering as a result. Workers were needed for the wall and the wall was the top priority.

Rob nodded. "Once the wall is finished, or as close to finished as possible, I'll give you back your guards. Until then, just make due with what you have."

He had also ordered the border checkpoints be set up with larger guard contingents, for both day and night. He even set up a tiny post at the Trog Pass, but more as a formality. No one would be allowed in or out without stating their name and business. These details were all logged on parchment provided by Zuthus and given to Saif for review.

Rob despised paperwork, most sane people did. But the encounter with the thief, sent by the thieve's guild, bolstered his resolve to have more control over who entered his kingdom. He may not be able to influence what they did once inside, but he wanted to know who was here. It wasn't a perfect system, but it was far better than nothing. And it gave him some sense of control, whether illusional or not.

Fenton nodded. Despite the stress he was under, he was handling it well. Rob could not help but feel proud of the young man. He had a lot of responsibility dumped on him in a relatively short amount of time, but he held his own.

Rob sighed. "And you're not going to like my new idea."

Fenton blanched, but quickly composed himself. "I can't wait to hear it, my lord."

Rob chuckled. "The passes at the southern end of the valley are relatively secured. But that leaves our entire eastern and western ranges. Anyone with the will and the means can cross over them and never be detected. We need eyes out there, watching for incursions."

The First Ward frowned. "I agree we are exposed, but the manpower situation is truly dire. Unless I can pull some people off working duties, I'll have no choice but to reduce the force on the border points."

It was as Rob suspected. But the wall was paramount, and he could only expect so much with so little. "Okay, we'll do this, then. Once I feel the wall is complete enough, I'll transfer some additional people to you. They are to be used to keep a lookout on who's passing over the ranges."

"Watchers of the Range," Fenton said with a knowing smile.

"The what of the what?"

"We can call them the Watchers of the Range, since that'll be their duty."

Rob thought of them as simply border guards, but the title did sound cool. "Alright, that's their official title, then."

"But where will we post them? I have absolutely no knowledge of the ranges, other than they're big and imposing."

"I'll work on it and have the information given to you. For now, I guess you can start looking for candidates from the workers whom you feel would fit the job."

They touched on some other issues and, when finished, Rob turned to leave.

"My lord, one last thing, before you go," Fenton said.

"Yes?" Rob caught himself sounding impatient, since he had so many other things to do. He needed to get in the habit of giving off the mystique of patience, even if he didn't feel it.

"I wanted to thank you for giving me this position of First Ward. In the beginning, I had no interest in it and wanted to go on adventures with you."

"And that can still happen, if you want it to."

"Well, that's the thing. I *really* like my duties now. The responsibility you've bestowed upon me has given me a renewed sense of purpose, and I don't want to change it. I'd like to stay on as the First Ward, if that is okay with you."

Rob smiled. "And what about a life of adventure? You were very keen on it." And, truth be told, the young man was very useful in a fight, despite his young age.

"This job gives me all the adventure I could want. There is so much to figure out and consider. And, I feel, it will only get more complex as the kingdom grows."

The kid is growing up fast. If only Rob had been that forward thinking at his age, life would be different. Then he realized where he was, and he quashed the reminiscing.

He put a hand on Fenton's shoulder. "You are the First Ward of Anika for as long as you want to be. Good enough?"

"Yes, my lord!" Fenton beamed. "And thank you!"

He left his First Ward with a renewed sense of security in his job, and went looking for Jace.

The no-longer-deceased man was cutting logs along the treeline beyond the east gate. He was shirtless and sheened in sweat, as he chopped the felled trees to the proper length Gunther required.

"So which do you prefer, woodcutter or woodsman?" Rob said after watching for a few minutes. He knew how much devastation Jace could cause with that ax.

The big man paused to wipe sweat from his brow and take a long pull from a waterskin.

"Depends on what I'm doing, I suppose," Jace said. "At the moment, I'm a woodcutter. Later, I'll be something else."

At least you're no longer a dead man, Rob wanted to say, but didn't. He was entirely sure how the joke would land. "Well, when you feel like being a woodsman, again, I have a job for you."

"I'm enjoying this job," Jace said, and returned to chopping.

"I was thinking of starting up a group of rangers to monitor the valley."

"Rangers. Isn't that an actual class?"

"Maybe, but I've yet to meet someone who identifies as one."

Jace kept chopping. "Then maybe you can create the class as your own. What do you mean by monitoring?"

Rob could sense Jace was intrigued. "Well, I imagine a ranger would combine the abilities of hunting, like a woodsman, and guarding the borders from people sneaking in."

"So a border guard, who hunts. Don't need to create a whole entire class for that."

"Okay, forget the class angle. But I do need people who can do that. Right now, no one is watching those mountains, and I have zero idea if a group of raiders is descending upon us at this moment."

Jace paused and turned to look at the eastern range. "Yes, I can understand your point. But it has been like that since the beginning. Why the sudden concern?"

Rob sighed. Up until now, he'd only told Saif of the risk of the raiders Peter warned him about. And he'd sworn Lessa to secrecy, even though the archer was totally indifferent.

He didn't want panic among the populace. There would be nothing to be gained from it, except problems. What urgency was needed would come from their king, whom they would obey.

But he needed Jace's help, so he told him about Peter and the raiders, along with his worries of an imminent invasion.

The big man listened and nodded, while stroking his beard.

"Okay, now I really understand why you've had a bee in your britches these past few days." He slammed the ax into a stump, nearly splitting it. "What do you want me to do?"

Rob gave him an overview of what he wanted. Basically, to find hunters, or train those with potential, to scout along the lengths of both ranges. Their job is to identify the most likely points people can cross and pass that on to Fenton.

"You don't want them to guard the passes?" Jace said.

"No, that will fall under Fenton's duties, once the wall is completed. Your rangers are meant to travel around the valley and watch for things."

"What things?"

"Good things, bad things, whatever. I can't be everywhere at once. Even though most of the traffic is along the main road, we have all this forest out there with no idea if they are full of new threats or not. That will be the ranger's duties.

"And the hunting?"

"They'll be out there on their own. The ability to sustain themselves would be needed. Granted, any point in the valley is less than a day's walk to a populated area, but since they'll already be in the forests, why not hunt, too?"

Jace stroked his beard and pondered for a few minutes.

Rob's impatience threatened to spike, but he wouldn't order Jace. He considered the man a friend.

"Okay, I'll do it," Jace finally said. "When do you want me to start?"

"Now, please, today. We can get others to chop wood."

"I like chopping, though," Jace said, and Rob feared he changed his mind.

Jace suddenly grinned. "But I like hunting more."

CHAPTER THREE

"A sewage system? I thought that was already taken care of," Rob said.

He and Saif were walking through Hope, checking on things and making sure everything was okay. Which they were, more or less. But the Sage had brought up installing a sewage system out of nowhere.

"My lord, every resident is using the outhouses behind their homes, or going out into the forest, next to the creek, to do their business. I thought, now that we have a working water system, we could consider the next step."

Rob pulled up his kingdom menu and looked at the resources needed. They were a lot. Even more than what had been used for the water supply.

"Is it really needed right now? There are a lot of other projects to start, once the wall is finished." Like another wall, but made from stone. Rob didn't mention it, though.

Saif adjusted his robes, a nervous habit he had when on the losing end of a debate. "It is a matter of sanitation. There are a fair number of people within Hope, and it is starting to get crowded. All of whom need a proper way to relieve themselves, and it is necessary for us to supply the means to rid the town of waste."

It did make sense, when explained that way, but Rob had become miserly with his limited resources. There was too much else that needed to get done, and a sewage system wasn't one of them. But he could see how serious Saif was, and he knew the sage was correct. It needed to be done.

"Okay, a sewage system then. Once the wall is finished, I'll allot workers and resources."

Saif said, "Could we have the covered option?"

Rob frowned and checked sewage options. It started with a simple, open sewer system, similar to what medieval towns had, where the sewage was channeled along the sides of the street and out of the town. There was an upgraded version, which allowed for stone slabs to be placed over the entirety of the system, with an improved pipe structure. Rob didn't need to have it explained to him why this was better.

"Covered it is then," he said.

"Thank you my lord. This will make the people very happy to hear."

A man approached them, smiling from ear to ear. "Lord Barron, might I have a moment of your time?"

"The king is very busy, at the moment," Saif said.

"No, it's okay. Let's hear what he wants." Rob was tired of talking about sewers.

"Thank you, my lord," the man said. "Allow me to introduce myself. My name is Smiley, and I have come here, to your fine kingdom, to spread joy and happiness to all its people."

Rob inwardly cringed. On second thought, maybe he would rather go back to talking about sewers. "How do you propose to accomplish that?"

Smiley's smile grew even bigger. "Booze, my lord. Lots and lots of booze!"

"Alcohol?" Rob said, suspect.

"That is a fancy way to describe ale, but, yes, alcohol. See, my family has been specializing in importing ale from suppliers from all over. We've been selling it from our wagon, but decided we needed a proper location to settle down and open the ultimate ale dispensary: a tavern! And, wouldn't luck just have it, we heard about your growing kingdom. And imagine my surprise to find there isn't a single tavern in the entire valley! A travesty, I say! A travesty of tavernly proportions!"

Rob gave Saif a sidelong look. "It sounds... interesting." Boozed up subjects. What could possibly go wrong?

To Rob's surprise, Saif liked the idea.

"It would make the people happy," Saif said. "Having access to a place they could relax in and drink an ale or two would do wonders for morale."

Disappointed he'd lost Saif's potential backing, Rob said, "So you have ale?"

Smiley nodded. "Yes, several casks in my wagon, just waiting to be consumed. And with more on the way, via my connections. The only thing is I would need your highness's permission to convert."

"Convert what?"

"My house into a tavern."

"You have a house, already? I thought they were all full." Not only were all the houses already taken and fully occupied, new arrivals were setting up shacks beyond the walls until new houses could be built.

Smiley said, "I bought one of the houses just yesterday from its owner, and at a fair price, I might add. And now I'd like to convert it into a little tavern, but that sort of thing needs your blessing, or so I am told."

Curious, Rob had Smiley show him his new home.

It was located not far from the town square, on a corner lot. A wagon, ladened with ale casks was parked outside. Several people were working on slowly removing the casks and wheeling them inside.

"My family," Smiley said by way of introduction. "Two sons and a daughter. All in the tavern business with their old pops!"

Having never converted a building before, Rob selected the house which surrounded it in a glowing outline, then called up its menu.

There was an option to convert to a tavern provided a tavern keeper was present. Interesting.

It also listed the required resources, which weren't much, considering a whole new building wasn't being constructed.

As if reading the resource list, too, Smiley said, "Any and all materials needed will be resourced by ourselves. Lumber, stone, nails, everything. We won't be taking anything that is currently needed elsewhere."

The numbers next to the list of resources all changed to 'nil', making Rob blink in surprise.

Smiley said, "And all money costs, which should go without saying."

The cost amount changed to 'nil', also.

Rob laughed. He wished all projects would change to nil. It would make things so much better.

A message appeared.

Approve converting this structure? Y/N.

He selected yes, and Smiley and his family cheered.

"Now we can get down to business," Smiley said. "But there is one tiny detail only you can help us with, my lord."

"And that would be?"

"Could you turn the building, so it faces the corner directly. That way we get the walking traffic from both streets."

Could he turn it? He selected the building again, but couldn't find an option to move anything.

Then something caught his eye. The final menu option was Demolish Structure, which showed a thirty percent recovery rate of used resources. Beneath that, was a sub-option called Delete Structure. It would instantly remove the structure from existence, with no resources recovered.

Why would he ever want to completely delete a building and not get some of its resources back?

"Is there no way to move it, my lord?" Saif asked.

Rob dismissed the menu. Then, impulsively, he raised his hands and made a motion, as if grabbing the outline around the house.

The building quivered, causing several roof tiles to fall off.

Aha!

Slowly, he rotated his hands and the building physically turned. He adjusted it so it faced the corner directly.

"How's that look?" Rob asked, enjoying this new ability.

Smiley said, "A little more to the right. That's it. A little more. Back left. There! Right there! Perfect!"

Rob released the outline.

Set structure here? Y/N.

He selected yes, and a puff of dust kicked up from under the building as it literally plopped into place.

"Thank you so much, my lord," Smiley said. "Okay, gang. Let's get this set up. I want to be serving tankards by tomorrow night!"

"That was impressive," Saif said. "I was unaware you had such powers."

"Neither did I, until now. Why would that be?"

Saif said, "You've mentioned before how some of the gods have been obscuring details of this world from you. Maybe that has changed."

Rob suspected he could have been repositioning erected structures this whole time, but only now was he aware of it. Could it be because his ally on the other side was helping him? Or it could be something unlocked when he leveled up the kingdom, but wasn't informed. He couldn't know for sure, but it was a positive improvement.

They watched Smiley's family as they went about converting the house. Adding a tavern to your fantasy town was a no brainer, but never once did Rob even consider it an option. What else was he missing out on?

What about an inn? Having a place to stay might invite merchants and people with specialties to visit.

He found the listing for an inn, but it required establishing the building on a new lot, and as long as an Innkeeper was present.

A message appeared.

You have been given a quest: Inn and Out.

Find an Innkeeper to establish an inn within Hope.
Reward: An Inn.

Rob sighed. He needed to stop poking around the kingdom menus so as to not get random quests.

Suddenly, Greta walked past, smiling and waving. "Hello, my lord!"

Rob nodded and turned to face Saif until she left from view. The woman still gave him the creeps, and it wasn't even her fault.

"Is there an issue with Greta, my lord?" Said said. "Has she been forcing her pies on you, again? I shall have a word with her."

"No, that's fine, Saif. And, no, there isn't an issue."

But there was. The message the voice had given him had been clear: get to the Ruins of the Dead City. Perhaps he'd been avoiding dealing with it by keeping himself busy with all the other things that needed his attention. But every time he saw Greta, which was several times a day, the message practically screamed into his ear.

He had to admit to himself, he couldn't avoid it much longer.

"I'm going to head out tomorrow morning," Rob said.

"Adventuring?"

"Dungeoning, if that's even a term. I have no idea how long I'll be gone, so you're in charge, as always."

"Very good, my lord. I'll make sure-." He stopped talking and stared over Rob's shoulder.

Rob turned to look.

A small group of horsemen were descending the castle hill, bearing Orbin's flag banners. Leading the group was Rob's Overlord: Quinn.

Momentarily stunned, Rob could only watch as the group reached level ground, then headed south along the road, until they rode out of view behind a line of wheat.

"He's leaving?" Rob said. "Do you know where?"

"Not at all. I've heard nothing about it."

That wasn't surprising. Orbin's men had absolutely no interactions with the townsfolk, beyond bossing them around, which suited Rob just fine. But this was the first time since Quinn's initial arrival that he'd seen the man leave the castle.

Castle.

Rob couldn't see any soldiers on the battlements or at the open gate. Could this mean King Orbin was abandoning his prized possession, and even the kingdom?

Needing to find out, he summoned Henry and rode up the steep incline. He passed through the gate and dismounted.

The courtyard still had tents and various items for cooking. But no horses or men.

He went inside the tower, heart racing.

It was still stocked with the supplies Quinn always hoarded. An empty wine bottle lay on its side upon the table the Overlord liked to get drunk.

Rob laughed. There was no one here.

Then he heard a voice, echoing off the stone walls. It came from the floor above.

He climbed the stairs, and found a soldier sitting at a desk. He was facing away from the stairs, and held an open locket in front of him. He appeared to be speaking to it.

"Yes, I understand," the soldier said to the locket. "I shall handle it."

Intrigued, Rob quietly walked closer. He was surprised when the locket suddenly spoke back.

"When he returns, he is to report in, immediately. He cannot take any actions without the proper approval."

Rob could finally see what the locket contained. It was the image of man, perhaps another soldier. He looked like he was standing in a room. Behind the man, lining several tables, were dozens of lockets on little stands.

"I'll make sure he does," said the soldier, and snapped the locket closed. He noticed Rob, and stood. "Yes, is something wrong?"

"Who are you?" Rob said. He didn't recognize him at all.

The man arched a brow. "The name is Flint. You must be King Barron. A pleasure to finally meet you." He shook Rob's hand.

A little stunned, Rob said. "I just saw Overlord Quinn leave. Where's he going?"

"On Overlord business, I suspect. He didn't tell me." He looked annoyed at the thought.

"So he's coming back?"

"He better, or he'll be in serious trouble if he doesn't. No need to look disappointed. You have plenty of reasons to hate the man, but he is your Overlord, and deserves your respect."

"Are you the only one here? Where are the rest of the soldiers?"

Flint looked thoughtful. "I suppose I am the only one here. But, not to worry, King Orbin is always watching."

"So you're a soldier, too?"

"I'm a soldier of a kind. The proper term for my job is..." He tried to find the right word. "Advisor! Yes, that's it. I'm an advisor to the Overlord. Now, if there was nothing else, I have a mountain of reports to review." He motioned to a pile of parchments on the desk.

Rob wondered what was on them. Reports on himself, and Anika? Had to be.

He was about to leave, then asked. "Hey, what was that thing you were talking into? I've never seen it before."

"Considering how underdeveloped your kingdom is, I'm not surprised," Flint said. "It's called a Speaking Mirror. Now, if you please." He shooed a hand for Rob to go.

Taking the hint, Rob left. But his mind was now full of more questions than answers.

CHAPTER FOUR

The next morning, Rob gathered up all his gear, as well as supplies. He was prepared for several days of exploration with extra potions, water and food.

What he had seen of the Dead City was huge; a sprawling mass of old stone buildings separated into several sections. He hadn't the opportunity at the time to really study it, since he was busy retrieving the Town Cornerstone. But he knew it couldn't be explored in a day or two.

After one last check-in with Saif, he made his way to the blacksmith's. Kortz was hammering away at a helmet when he walked in. All along the walls were stacks of rectangular, iron ingots, ready to be turned into armor and weapons.

"Good morning, my lord," Kortz said. "You are just in time. Here, a present for you." He handed Rob the helmet.

Steel helmet.

Armor: 15

Value: 100 gold pieces

"Very nice," Rob said. It had almost double the armor as his previous one, which he'd lost after his last death.

He slipped it on. "Feels comfortable, too."

"Paxx added a donkey hide lining, so it should be snug. And I have this ready, too." He pulled a gleaming steel shield from the wall.

Rob slipped his arm through its handles.

Steel Shield of Evasion.

Block: +14%

Dexterity: +3

Value: 500 Gold Pieces.

Rob whistled at the stats. An actual Dexterity boost. That would certainly help with his dodging.

"This is fantastic, Kortz. Thank you."

"Imagine my surprise when forging it triggered my anvil's tiny chance of imbuing a magical trait, but there's bad news to go along with the good."

"And that is?"

"I used the last of our steel on those. We're all out, and down to just iron."

"So you need more steel, then?"

"Well, sure, as a stopgap solution. What we really need is a source of tin to mix with all this iron we have. That would get us all the steel you would need."

"And where do you find tin?"

"In the ground, if the gods truly bless you. Tin mines are one of the rarest types out there. If you don't have a tin mine, then you'll have to buy tin from someone who does."

You have been given a quest: Tin and Tinner.

Locate a reliable source of tin for the blacksmith.

Reward: 5,000 experience points.

Rob frowned at the unimaginative quest name, but liked the amount of experience points. It looked like finding a source was going to be difficult.

He spotted his Buckler of Bashing leaning against the wall, all bent out of shape from the bull charge it had absorbed. "Any chance the Shield Bash bonus on that can be salvaged?"

Kortz picked it up and looked it over. "The buckler materials could maybe be salvaged, but the enchantment can't be. You would need an Enchanter to transfer it, and a competent one at that."

You have been given a quest: Enchanter or Bust.

Find an Enchanter to join your kingdom, and gain access to enchantments which can be imbued upon items.

Reward: 15,000 experience points.

Rob whistled at the reward amount. The quest looked more difficult than the tin one.

"I heard you and Lessa are jumping into a dungeon today."

"Yes, hopefully I'll find some tin for you in it."

Kortz laughed. "I'd prefer treasure, or a new anvil."

Rob went looking for Lessa and found her atop the battlements on the southern wall. She was barking orders at a half dozen archer trainees.

He climbed a ladder, and watched. The battlements were haphazard in construction, made simply from some split logs held up by wooden brackets. Not ideal, but it gave defenders a view over the wall.

Below, several scarecrows made of straw had been placed at intervals. He noted there were more arrows on the ground than in the scarecrows.

Lessa raised her arm, and the archers drew their bows. "Ready! Aim! Fire!"

Arrows arched through the air, but only one connected with a target.

"Again!" Lessa shouted.

"Are they improving?" Rob asked as he approached.

"Some are, some aren't. For the moment, it's less about the aim than it is about developing the specific muscles to draw and shoot. Both will take time."

"I'm ready to go, if you are."

"I'm always ready for some excitement."

"What about your supplies?"

She nodded at her full pack leaning against the wall. "Been ready since before dawn. Just been killing time until you crawled out of your cot."

"Ha ha. Very funny."

She turned to the trainees. "I want you to do this all day, everyday. You'll only stop when I return or if your arms fall off!"

In unison, the trainees shouted, "Yes, Commander!"

She put on her pack, and adjusted the placement of her quivor, which was stuffed full of arrows.

"So, you're a Commander now?" Rob teased.

"They were calling me Master, before, but I didn't think it was respectful enough. Are we leaving?"

Rob summoned and mounted Henry, then rode through the southern entrance. Lessa easily kept pace alongside, thanks to her running ability.

They immediately turned off the road and headed east along a well worn path. As they passed by the wall, the trainees cheered. As did the people who were working on the wall.

"I'm beginning to think they're really happy to see me leave," Rob said. He summoned his shale-mites and the two appeared in the air, flying on either side.

"I know my trainees are happy. Now there's no one to boss them around."

They rode for a while, then turned south into the forest, slowing their pace.

At one point, they passed a woman crouched in a tree, a sword across her back. Rob recognized her from town.

"Are you a ranger?" Rob called out as they rode by.

"Yes, my lord! The first!" she said, and waved.

Rob was happy to see Jace wasn't waiting around. He'd managed to find a skilled woodswoman, and already had her nosing about the valley.

"What's a ranger?" Lessa said, as she ran alongside him. She was barely breathing heavily.

"Eyes and ears of the valley. When we're busy below ground, they'll be watching things up top."

"Why was she up a tree?"

"Don't know, don't care."

They soon reached the northern edge of the swamp. A fine mist clung to the ground as it scudded along the surface.

Rob dismounted, and despawned Henry. "We're close. The entrance is just up ahead," he said quietly.

"Why the hushed tone?"

"Quartek hangs out in a pond just over there. We *definitely* don't want to attract his attention."

"He's the reason you put a ban on anyone hunting in the swamps?"

"Him, and the northern end of Annex Marsh just to our south. Both are problems we don't need right now."

"Or ever," Lessa said.

But Rob knew that wasn't true. Both were on his ever growing to-do list.

They picked their way through the swamp, with the shale-mites scouting ahead. Soon, the cave entrance came into view, located at the base of a large tree.

It had been a while since Rob had been there, and the place looked as creepy as ever.

After taking a few moments to watch the entrance for any surprises, or new inhabitants, they went in.

Casting Light, they kept their weapons at the ready, and Rob sent the mites in ahead.

They walked until the first side tunnel was reached. Down it was the chamber of the being who called himself the Watcher. Or it was some jerk on the outside, who enjoyed messing with Rob.

Regardless, he didn't want anything to do with whatever the Watcher was peddling.

"Just a sec," Rob said, and fished a stone out of a pouch. He slapped it against the side of the tunnel entrance, and stone began to morph and grow over it. Soon, the entrance was completely sealed with stone.

"Why did you do that?" Lessa asked.

"For peace of mind."

They continued, and reached the final side tunnel entrance.

"The city is down that way, but I want to check something first."

"More peace of mind."

"Let's just say I don't want any surprises."

He led them down the remainder of the main tunnel until they reached the small chamber at the end. This had been the lair of the Rat Queen which Rob had slain so long ago. It had been one of his first big quests.

Their light spells easily illuminated the space, revealing nothing new. Rob had been worried the game would have stuck something nasty in here. Perhaps something that would impede his further exploration of the tunnels. But there wasn't anything to worry about.

They returned to the side tunnel and took it.

"Hard to believe there's an entire city down here," Lessa said after a few minutes of steady descent. She kept looking back, watching their rear.

"You should be able to get a gander at it in a few minutes. Sort of an overview of what we're in for."

"Giving me a chance to change my mind?"

"There's no changing it now, I'm afraid."

"That's too bad. I wanted to go back to being called Commander."

They eventually reached the point in the tunnel with the strange hole in the wall.

Pausing for a break, Rob looked through it.

The hole was very short and opened up into a vast chamber beyond.

Only something was different.

"Hey, wait a second," Rob said.

The chamber wasn't dark at all, but brightly lit. Why was that?

"Problem?"

Rob sent one of the shale-mites through to check the other side. "Yes. The last time I was here, the chamber lighting didn't activate until I entered it. But it's light in there, now."

Lessa frowned. "So, someone else is in there?"

"If that's how the light stuff works, yeah. Or it could just always be like that."

Rob didn't like this change. It gave an even bigger sense of foreboding to the place.

"Shall we take a look? You said there was a ledge on the other side?" Lessa said.

"Yeah, be careful."

"Always."

Dropping her gear, Lessa hoisted herself up and climbed through. After a few minutes, she returned.

"Whatcha think?" Rob asked as she redawned her gear.

"Creepy. Very creepy. Maybe I will go back to town."

Curious if anything else was different, Rob climbed through to the other end. Sticking his head out, he could see the city spread out before him, far below. It was considerably brighter than the last time, giving him a clearer view of areas previously masked by darkness.

Stone buildings were crammed up against each other, and narrow streets snaked between them. The sections of the city were more distinct, with some even walled off, like a gated community. At one end was what appeared to be a large dome, as big as an entire city section. Another section, against the far wall of the massive cavern, was composed almost entirely of towers of varying heights, like giant, handmade stalagmites.

The city continued out of view to his right.

He looked down at the ledge, and far below that was a street going along the wall. He guessed he was well over a hundred feet above the bottom of the cavern, but couldn't be sure.

He sat and stared at the city, looking for any movement. He focussed on cross-streets where he was most likely to spot someone.

After a while of seeing and hearing nothing, he crawled back.

"Anything?" Lessa said as he reclaimed his gear.

"Just a lot to explore. I wonder who built it."

"I'm more concerned with why they left. It's a dungeon now, so that can't be good."

They continued on. The tunnel alternated between a long flight of narrow, carved stairs, and a long, narrow straight away.

But soon they came upon another side tunnel, going to the right.

"This was as far as I got last time," Rob said. "I figure if we stay on this main tunnel, we'll eventually reach the city. But I can't leave this behind us without checking it out."

Lessa nodded, and they turned off into the side tunnel.

Almost immediately, it came to an end at a flat wall.

"That was anticlimactic," Lessa said.

Not wanting to give in, Rob scrutinized the wall. He could barely make out something engraved upon it. Using the tip of his dagger, he scratched at the engraving. It was the shape of a heart, right at the center of the wall.

"How romantic," Lessa said.

"If this place is anything, it is not romantic." But what did it mean, and why was it here?

Stumped, Rob pushed at the heart with the dagger's pommel.

Instantly, the heart turned a bright, ruby red. Then the wall suddenly slid to the side, making them jump back in alarm.

Not a wall; a door.

A rocky chamber had opened up to them. Careful to not cross the threshold, Rob peered around.

At one side was a large humanoid statue, kneeling on one knee, head down with its fists thrust before it.

On the other was a small monolith looking rock sticking out of the floor.

Glowing crystals lined the walls and vaulted ceiling, lighting up the entire space.

Rob sent in the mites, one to the statue, the other the monolith.

The huge bugs landed on their respective targets and crawled around. Nothing happened.

"Whatcha think?" Lessa said. "Trap or test?"

"Maybe a test that traps."

"Or a trap that tests."

"Either way, this place is here for a reason."

"What reason would that be?" Lessa said.

"Me," Rob said, and stepped into the chamber.

As he did, a line of glowing, red hearts appeared on the floor in front of him. They went across the room, lighting up one by one, until they stopped in front of the monolith.

"Maybe you should stay out there," Rob said.

"What good would that do when the door closes. And you know it's going to close, and it won't open for me. That's how these things work, right?" She stepped into the room. The door didn't close.

Rob followed the line, keeping one eye on the statue. When he got to the monolith, he shooed the shale-mite away and looked it over.

A heart shaped hollow was carved straight through its width to the other side. The heart was the same size as the ones on the floor and door.

Using the dagger, he tapped at the monolith's surface. He then slowly inserted the blade up to the hilt. Nothing happened.

He went to the statue and examined it. It was twice the size as him, but devoid of any real details, like a mannequin. Within its clenched fists, held like a sword, was a narrow stone cylinder. Its end was shaped like a heart.

Lessa looked from the cylinder, to the hole in the monolith. "Wow. What a difficult puzzle," she deadpanned. "I wonder if we'll ever solve it."

Rob exchanged the dagger for his sword. He then reached for the cylinder.

Lessa put a hand on his shoulder, stopping him. "You know the moment you touch that, things are going to get exciting real quick."

"I thought you liked excitement?" Rob said, and with his shield hand, grasped the cylinder.

A sudden grinding noise made them turn.

The door quickly slid closed, trapping them inside.

"I knew it!" Lessa said.

The statue suddenly yanked the cylinder out of Rob's grasp.

The two quickly backpedaled to the other side of the chamber, as the statue stood.

Raising its head revealed a smooth, featureless surface. But a pair of arrows suddenly sprouted from its face.

"I figure go for the head," Lessa said, knocking another arrow.

Rob hit it with a level two Sun Bolt, which etched a wide scar across its chest.

The thing didn't even appear to register the attacks, and walked towards them with the cylinder clasped in one fist, and the other raised for smashing.

Rob sicked the mites on it, and the bugs attacked, flying around it and swooping in to bite.

The statue suddenly lunged and brought its large fist down, glancing off of Rob's shield as he barely dodged out of the way, and striking the ground.

Rob looked at the savage crater it created. One direct strike could instantly kill either of them. "Stay out of its range!"

"No kidding," Lessa said, as she fired a rapid volley while moving backwards. She positioned herself behind the monolith and kept shooting.

As the statue swung a haymaker at him, Rob rolled under it, then swung down hard at its arm. A loud clang filled the chamber, and Rob noticed he'd actually cut a few inches into its stone. But the thing didn't register any damage. It kept on mindlessly attacking.

For several minutes, they fought. Every move the pair made was calculated to stay away from that deadly fist. They managed it, all the while peppering it with arrows and the occasional sword strike.

At one point, during a dodge, Rob found himself within the being's guard. Instincts took over, and he lunged forward with a shield bash.

CLANG!

He stumbled back, head spinning. It was like running right into a wall.

"Watch out!" Lessa shouted.

Rob barely heard her over the resonating gong noise in his ears. He had a perception of a boulder falling towards his skull.

As the boulder fell, he felt himself being yanked away by the scruff of his mail shirt.

Lessa pulled him back behind the monolith. She'd used her running ability to quickly snatch him. "No more shield bashing!" she shouted and led the statue away to the other side of the chamber.

For a grueling amount of time, they fought and dodged. Eventually, the entire floor was covered with impact craters. But the statue had taken damage. It's smooth body had been chipped away to the point nearly half of its stone had been removed.

Finally, it made a lunge at Lessa, but collapsed to the floor. As it tried to push itself up, Rob shouted and brought his sword down with all his might, breaking off its head.

The statue went still and suddenly crumbled apart to nothing. All that remained was the fist clutching the cylinder.

"Now that was a work out," Lessa said, wiping sweat from her brow. Her quivor was nearly empty, and would need time to regenerate more arrows.

The door slid open.

Rob took a breather, spitting out dust and bits of stone he'd inhaled. "It was like trying to downsize a mountain," he said, before quaffing a health potion.

"A mountain which fought back. You going to do the honors?"

Tensed up for deceit, he grasped the end of the cylinder. The stone fist crumbled away, releasing it.

Rob went over to the monolith, and carefully slid it into place.

The heart shape of the cylinder turned ruby red.

A message appeared.

Touch for a permanent, one time, 25 hit point maximum increase for you and all members of your party.

Rob whistled.

"What? What is it?" Since she wasn't the Chosen One, she couldn't see the message.

"A welcome boost. Check this out." Rob put his hand against the glowing heart.

You have gained +25 to your maximum hit points.

Nice. Rob marveled at the boost. Would the city have more?

"Okay, that made this entire morning worth it," Lessa said with a grin. "Usually you have to level, or find an imbued item to get anything close to such a gain."

Rob grinned. "Let's go see what else is in store for us."

CHAPTER FIVE

After taking a few minutes to recover, and brush dust and bits of statue off themselves, they returned to the main tunnel. Both the shale-mites had been killed, so Rob had no way of scouting ahead, as the mites couldn't be resummoned for another twenty four hours.

"We need to take it slow from here on out," he said.

Cautious, they moved forward. The tunnel kept alternating between stairs and hallways, without any discerning features to give them a sense of the distance they were traveling.

In his mind, Rob tried to place them in the wall from where the viewing hole had been. The chamber was so immense, and the walls encompassing it so vast, he couldn't do it.

Then, the straight hallway they were on didn't become a set of descending stairs. It kept going, and even started to curve to the left. It was a meager sign of progress, but Rob would take it. He was sick of stairs.

"Think we're on the ground level of the city?" Lessa said in a hushed voice. Every sound they made was magnified in this place.

"Probably. Don't jinx us."

Suddenly, ahead, light from their spell showed the hallway open up.

They stopped, wary, and on full alert.

Rob moved to the terminus of the hall and looked around.

It was a large, dark chamber with walls barely discernible at the edges of their light.

"Hello?" Rob called out, and Lessa lightly elbowed his back.

"Hey, we need to be quiet, right?" she said.

"If anything is here, it could hear us coming from way back."

They entered, heads swiveling for a potential attack.

Their light revealed a pair of huge, stone doors on the left wall. They were easily three times Rob's height, and wide enough to ride four wagons abreast through.

Above the doors, carved in stone, was a set of large hieroglyphs.

Rob said, "Any idea what it says?'

"No idea. I'm not fluent in gibberish. Maybe something about all will die who dare to enter."

"Or it's the name of the city."

He looked at the doors more closely. They were solid stone and incredibly smooth. The seam between them was barely discernible. Air tight.

Directly in the middle, between them, was a small, diamond shaped indentation barely an inch deep.

Rob probed it with his dagger but nothing happened. "What's this for?"

"A key, maybe?"

They searched around the room for anything which might be a key, but only found dust and bits of debris.

"Well, what do we do now? Any idea where to look for the key?" Lessa said, as she checked on her quivor. It was almost full, again.

"Not a clue," he said, frustrated. He examined the indentation, again, scratching at it with his finger. Encrusted dust broke out of it, revealing more of its form. He recognized it. It was identical to the keyhole on the tomb which required a death shard to open.

He checked his pouches, but realized he'd given all his shards to Unger for making spell stones. "You wouldn't happen to have a shard on you?"

"No, nothing. We could go back to town and-."

A loud hissing sound interrupted her.

They looked around, trying to locate the source, but the echoing in the room was terrible.

"I don't like this," Lessa said.

Then, movement on the back wall caught their attention. Large shapes were crawling down it.

Alarmed, Rob said, "Back to the tunnel. Now!"

As they ran to the tunnel entrance, their light moved with them, revealing more of the moving shapes.

Huge spiders, covered in greenish-brown fur. To Rob, they resembled wolf spiders. About a dozen scampered down the wall and across the floor at them.

Lessa was already firing volleys before they'd reached the entrance, and Rob cast sun bolt.

Once in the hall, they turned to meet their enemy.

Spiders ran at them, forced by the narrowness of the tunnel to crawl over each other.

Shield in front, Rob swung and jabbed. The massive arachnids hissed with each hit, but kept coming.

Over his shoulder, Lessa rapidly fired arrows into the growing mass of hairy bodies.

Suddenly, a spider bigger than the others, pushed through. Huge mandibles arced upwards, dripping with venom.

Rob and Lessa quickly backed up, as the monster squeezed itself into the tunnel to get at them.

"Mana gone!" he shouted as he cast his last sun bolt, the cheaper, level one version. But he couldn't quaff a potion while locked into combat.

The monster spider was the stuff of nightmares; a smaller, yet, just as terrifying version of the Goliath Tarantula he encountered in the Annex Marsh.

The spider horde, led by the giant, pushed them further and further back.

Then, as if by some unheard signal, they suddenly turned around and scurried down the tunnel, until all that could be heard was their distant, echoing hissing.

Rob and Lessa leaned against the wall, panting and sweating.

"I didn't think they would make this easy," Rob said.

"Evil gods?"

"Yeah," Rob said after thinking how to properly answer. More like evil programmers.

After a few minutes to recover, and drink the required potions, Lessa said, "Back to town? Grab that shard?"

Rob shook his head. "It would give time for the whole nest to respawn. I think the big one was summoning them, but couldn't really tell." The chaos in the tunnel had been horrific. "We kill the mother, and then we don't have to do this all over again."

Lessa stood. "Works for me."

They went back to the room, the sounds of the hissing getting louder. As they got close enough to see the entrance, the spiders surges through it.

This time, though, they were less in number, and the mother spider still had a dozen arrows bristling from its body.

Sticking with what worked, the two of them backed up, hacking and shooting. Eventually, nearly all the smaller ones were dead, and the mother was severely injured.

As if sensing it was in trouble, it spun about, and retreated.

They followed quickly behind, Lessa firing continuously.

The spider made it back into the room, but its injuries were so numerous, it collapsed in the middle of the floor.

Rob leapt forward and ran his sword through the middle of its cluster of eyes. The thing shuddered, its legs curling under it, then went still.

Removing his helmet, Rob wiped sweat from his forehead. "This place needs air conditioning."

"What's air conditioning?"

"Nothing." He spotted the twinkle of an item tucked beneath the dead spider's body and scooped it up.

You have taken an item: Medium Shard of Nature Magic.

"And here is our key," Rob said.

"Let's give it a second, okay?" Lessa said as she went to sit against the wall, kicking a dead spider out of the way.

Rob did the same, twirling the shard in his hands. So much in this world depended on these things, and yet, there was never nearly enough. He hoped there would be more inside the city. Especially the Life Magic variety. He knew Jace wouldn't be the last death of significance he'd have to contend with. The more Life Magic shards the better for his conscience. He wanted a hoard of them as backup.

Once they'd fully rested, they stood before the double doors.

"Ready?" Rob asked.

Lessa stood to one side, arrow drawn. "Yeah, sure."

Rob slid the shard into the slot, fitting perfectly with a loud click.

The doors swung open.

CHAPTER SIX

The huge stone doors swung inward, forcing them to back up. The moment a space between the doors appeared, a sudden gust of wind blasted out of the side tunnel and whipped through the opening doors. Rob and Lessa were forced to shield their eyes from the buffeting wind. After a full minute, the wind died down and they could look.

The cavern was opened before them, albeit from a lower angle than the hole from before. A wide, stone street went straight ahead as far as they could see. To the left side was the natural wall of the cavern, studded with glowing rocks, and bright fans of fungi of various colors. It continued on for several hundred paces until ending at a cross street, which went left. On the right side, single story stone buildings lined the street, blocked off by a high wall which was capped by a bristling line of white, spiky crystals.

In the distance, a portion of one of the domes could be seen, as well as a part of the section of the city made of towers.

Rob and Lessa waited just within the doorway, wary of an attack. All that could be heard were the sounds of their own tense breathing. The dead city was as silent as a tomb.

When he was certain nothing would happen, Rob poked his head out, checking to either side, but saw nothing to be alarmed about. They crossed through the doorway, and stood in the street.

Quest Complete: Exploring You Shall Go.

You have found an entryway into the Ruins of the Dead City. Explore it, but use caution. Not everything may be dead.

Reward: 1,000 experience points.

"There's no welcoming committee, so that's good," Rob said.

Lessa glanced behind them and up, then blanched.

Rob looked back. The cavern wall went up from the doorway. Because of all the glowing crystals and fungi on its surface, they could see it vault upward; up and up and up, until they could make out the roof.

Rob was suddenly hit with a bout of vertigo, and quickly looked away, fighting off a dizzy spell.

Lessa said, "Are you okay?"

"Yup," Rob said, bent over and bracing his knees with his knuckles. How silly would he have looked had he dropped his sword and shield? He'd never been within a structure so colossal before. Not even the domed stadiums back home could hope to compare to this. He was feeling the reverse of a claustrophobic attack, but managed to get it under control.

"I'm good," he said, straightening up. "I just won't look up."

With the cavern wall on their left and the high wall to the right, the only option was to go forward along the street.

"This isn't the main entrance," Rob said. "It must be somewhere else." The quest message said this was an entryway, indicating more than one.

"It's too boring to be the main entrance," Lessa said. "Usually cities open up to a market area."

Whatever markets existed here were long gone. The only thing left was silence and a natural feeling of eeriness.

They slowly started walking, and became alarmed at the sound of their footfalls which echoed off of everything. But, since going barefoot wasn't an option, they continued.

After a hundred paces, a sudden grinding noise made them spin about.

The stone doors were slowly closing.

Rob cursed, summoned Henry, then raced back, the hoofbeats sounding like cannonfire on the stone ground.

But the door closed with an audible thump before he could reach it. Dismounting, he pushed at its surface, but it didn't budge.

Lessa ran up to him. "Now, we had to have expected that to happen, right?"

Rob sighed. "I guess. Look, there's a shard keyhole on this side, as well."

There was a diamond shaped hole between the door seams. All they needed to do was find another medium shard to get out.

"We're truly committed now," Lessa said.

They both were thinking the same thing. They'd brought a week's worth of supplies with them, most of which was packed into Henry's saddlebags. Although they were now locked in there was time to find a way out.

As they went back down the street, again, Rob was forced to despawn Henry. The animal's hoofs were simply creating way too much noise, making them even more nervous.

When they got to the farthest point as before, Rob paused. "What's that crap on the wall?" He pointed at the white spiky crystals. The wall didn't have a break or opening in it for as far as he could see.

"No clue, but it looks nasty."

They stepped off the street onto a wide walkway. The wall was seamless, as if formed out of the stoney ground, easily ten or twelve feet high, and impossible to vault over because of the bristling spikes, which looked razor sharp. There was no way over. Rob wished he could summon his shale-mites to fly over and see what happened.

"Keep out," Lessa said. "Looking at the length, this wall runs all the way to the other side of the cavern. Effectively closing off over half the city."

But why? Rob knew the game liked to 'wall off' areas which were too difficult for his current level. Maybe this was more of that. No matter, there was still a vast portion of the city to explore.

They continued walking, until they reached where the cavern wall on the left ended, forming a T-junction. The new road followed along the cavern wall, leading to more buildings. The section with the huge dome and towers could be seen more clearly, as well as other blocks of structures ahead and to the right. They shared some common features; all appeared to have been carved directly out of stone, and all were in complete ruin. Many of the roofs and walls had collapsed, or were on the brink, making the prospect of entering them more than a little concerning.

Everything was marbled with veins of glowing rocks, or covered in ephemeral fungi, lighting up the entire cavern. It gave Rob the feeling of being in one of those big box stores with their phosphorus lights.

They stood at the junction, taking it all in. There had to be thousands of buildings, just in this section of the city, alone. The roofs of many thousands more could be seen beyond the sectioning wall.

"Which way?" Lessa said.

"Let's turn off here."

As they changed direction, and began to walk up the new road, Lessa held up a hand and they froze.

A distinct grinding noise could be heard, coming from somewhere within the buildings next to them. These weren't walled off, and their empty doorways and windows seemed to stare at them like the eyes of the dead.

"That your stomach?" Lessa said.

"No." He couldn't make out the exact location the sound was coming from.

The grinding stopped for a few moments, then continued.

Lessa focused on the sound, and pointed toward a narrow space between two crumbling buildings.

Rob cautiously walked over to get a better angle, and saw that the space made an alleyway which went deeper amongst the buildings. He looked to Lessa, who shrugged.

Sighing, he led them into the space, following the sound.

The alleyway branched off many times, revealing a network of narrow corridors leading from the main street. Each doorway or window they passed had to be done so with caution, as every building presented a potential ambush point, making progress slow.

But soon the narrow alley opened up to a large, open section between buildings, revealing the source of the sound.

A huge grub-like creature was on the wall of a building. Its coloring matched the stone and even had a colorful, glowing pattern on its long back, resembling the crystals around them. Triangular mandibles munched the fungus on the wall, and it paused occasionally to suck it in. A long, cleared path showed where it had already eaten its way along the wall.

Rob looked at its name: Cave Grub.

The thing didn't react to their presence, it just kept munching away on the fungus.

"What should we do?" Lessa asked.

"About that? It seems to be doing a service, keeping the walls clean."

Suddenly, another noise could be heard. A loud skittering sound. The grub seemed to sense it, too, and stopped eating. The confined space of the alley made the noise sound like it was coming from everywhere.

Antennas appeared on the roof of the building, swiveling and probing. Rob and Lessa backed up.

A massive ant crawled into view and looked down from the roof's edge. It was as big as a large dog, with a pair of long, jagged pincers protruding from its jaws.

The skittering continued and three more ants appeared.

"Maybe we should go," Lessa said.

The ants, having found their prey, quickly climbed down the wall and attacked the cave grub.

The grub hissed, and strange nodules unfolded on its back. It suddenly squirted a gray liquid from the nodules, hitting the ants.

One ant twitched uncontrollably, as the liquid ate away at its exoskeleton and forming huge bubbles.

More ants appeared.

Time to go.

Rob and Lessa ran back down the alley, the sounds of hissing and skittering continuing behind them. Once they reached the street again, they stopped and looked back. Nothing pursued them.

"Well, that was terrifying," Lessa said, looking shaken.

Rob envisioned being swarmed by a horde of those mutant ants and shivered. How many of those things could be in here with them?

They continued along, more wary than before. The street ran along the vast cavern wall and occasionally branched off with other streets which Rob chose to ignore for now. There was something at the far end of the street that intrigued him.

The huge dome loomed large at the back of the city, and the street led them directly to it. Built up from a sunken depression, the massive structure resembled a wide, flattened mushroom. Several open entryways dotted its base. From those streamed out mutant ants. Hundreds and hundreds of them.

"Well, looks like we found their nest," Lessa said, turning to leave. "We'll stay way clear of this part of the city."

But Rob wasn't in any hurry to go. "Hang on a second." He scanned over the dome and found several narrow stairways carved into its sides. Each led up to a small entrance from which no ants came or went.

Lessa spotted them, too. "Oh, no. You're not thinking of trying to have a look, are you?"

He was. This was the single largest building in the whole, viewable cavern. The game had it there for a purpose.

Could it contain the exploit?

"I just want to take a quick peek," he said, "You can stay back, and cover me as I climb up."

Lessa shook her head. "I want to go on record saying that this is a terrible idea."

"You're probably right," Rob said, and headed down into the depression.

Careful to avoid detection, Rob followed a wide set of stairs until he reached the very bottom. The ants were mostly concentrated near the front entryways, and appeared to be blind or near sighted.

He hurried over to the building's wall. A stairway was carved into it, each step barely a foothold. With a quick look around, and up at his worried archer, he climbed.

The going was slow, but after several long minutes, he reached the top. He was easily a hundred feet up the wall; a fall from this height would send him back to the resurrection chamber in Hope.

Canceling his Light spell, he went inside. The entryway was small, forcing him to crouch, and went deeper inside.

The sounds of scuttling and clacking echoed from directly ahead, and he finally could see the other end. A large open space could be seen beyond.

He carefully approached the end of the tunnel, and slowly peeked out of it.

The dome was completely hollowed out, and resembled a stadium back in the real world. All along its side were glowing rocks and spirals of bright fungi.

Down below, on the ground level, were hundreds of mutant ants. At the very center, upon a mound of debris, was a monstrous slug-like creature. A pair of comically huge mandibles protruded from one end, along with a pair of huge antenni, like telephone poles.

The queen.

As he watched, her body suddenly quivered, and several long, white eggs emerged from her massive body and were taken away by workers.

Rob shivered at the horrific tableau. Lessa was right, they would stay clear of the dome, and focus their explorations on other parts of the city. No need to deal with this.

But as he turned to go, a message appeared, almost startling him.

You have been given a quest: Pest Control.

Clear the dome of ants, and their queen. Doing so will grant you access to the Garden beyond.

Reward: 5,000 Experience Points.

Rob sighed. He knew it. He knew the game wouldn't let him avoid this nightmare. But what garden?

He peered about and spotted a narrow entrance, way at the back of the dome. A soft light emanated from within. Something was inside. There was no way of reaching it without killing everything in the dome. Figured.

He couldn't be sure whether the quest was essential or not. But the exploit was somewhere in the city and every room, or ant filled dome, had to be checked.

Annoyed, Rob turned back to give Lessa the bad news.

CHAPTER SEVEN

She didn't take it well.

"I knew it!" she said, visibly upset. "The moment you said you wanted to have a look, I knew it wouldn't be a good thing."

The two of them had snuck away from the dome and back to the street without being detected.

"We don't have to do anything about them, right now. We still have a city to explore." Rob felt genuinely bad for Lessa. It was obvious she didn't like insects, especially the mutant variety. She only tolerated Rob's shale-mites because they could be controlled.

The archer sighed, then shrugged in defeat. "Fine. Where to now?"

"Back to that intersection, again. We'll take the other way."

"Not interested in what could be inside these buildings?"

"Yeah, but first, I need to get a better idea of the layout of this place. Once we do, then we can start to hit these buildings."

They walked back down the street with Lessa looking around, a little nervous.

Rob wasn't used to seeing her like this. She was always calm and cool, almost detached. But the ants changed that.

After a short distance, Rob realized something, and looked up. Almost instantly, he felt his vertigo start to overwhelm him, but he managed to keep it in check. His eyes climbed up the massive wall.

"What? What is it?" Lessa said, slightly alarmed.

Rob stepped back, away from the wall, to get a better look. Then he spotted it.

"The hole from the hallway," he said, pointing at it high above.

Lessa wasn't impressed, and kept her eyes on the nearby buildings.

Rob shifted over until he was directly in line with the hole, then went up to the wall. He searched around the mounds of broken rocks.

Lessa said, "What are you looking for? Did you drop something before?"

"In a manner of speaking," Rob said, then found what he was looking for.

"What?"

He scooped up a skull from the ground. It was severely cracked, and missing a large piece at the back. "An old friend."

This was from the skeleton which had the Town Cornerstone. The one whose eyes had appeared, and a voice mocked him.

Who had it been? A programmer? Had they been the ones to take control of the ogre at the mine? Were they watching him now, hoping he would fail? Probably. Rob felt they wouldn't be pleased with the progress he'd made since then.

Maybe they would appear here, again, to taunt him. He wanted them to. Anything they said could be something important or revealing.

He stared at the empty sockets for several minutes, willing his enemy to appear, but nothing happened. The eye sockets remained hollow and empty.

"Are you okay?"

Lessa's voice brought him out of his trance-like focus. "Just fine," he said, then hurled the skull over the buildings. They heard it shatter.

"Okay, let's go," Rob said, returning to the street.

They reached the three-way intersection without incident. After a quick check of the surroundings, and the closed doors, they followed the new direction.

For several minutes, it was more of the same: empty, crumbling buildings to the left, and the high wall sectioning off the city to the right. In the distance, against the opposite cavern wall, the cluster of towers grew closer.

Then, Lessa spotted something.

"There's a large gap in the wall ahead."

Intrigued, they approached the gap with caution. It was actually a large, open courtyard leading off from the street. The spiked wall looped around the courtyard, then continued on toward the towers. At the far side was a familiar sight.

"I think it's another of those statues," Lessa said, squinting. The open area was big enough to hold another dome, and the statue's detail was hard to make out. "More health rewards?"

"Let's find out," Rob said.

The pair walked across the massive courtyard. Being out in such a vast space made Rob feel exposed. But if anything did try to attack, they'd certainly see it coming.

Reaching what he felt was a safe distance, they stopped and peered at the statue.

It was nearly identical to the one they'd fought before, only larger. Easily twice the size. It was kneeling on one knee, and instead of holding a stone rod, its huge fists were touching the ground.

Engraved deeply in its wide chest was a narrow ring with what looked to be clasped hands at the top.

"Do you know what that symbol is?" Rob said. His hands gripped his sword tightly. The giant thing made him nervous.

"Nope. It's definitely not a heart, so no health bonus from this thing."

Behind the statue, a large gate made of double doors was set into the wall. The top of which bristled with white spikes.

Rob walked around the statue, giving it a wide berth, and inspected the gate. Unlike the cavern doors, this didn't have a shard-shaped keyhole, or a keyhole of any kind. The gate appeared to lead into the closed off part of the city.

"Anything?" Lessa said.

"No," Rob said, placing his shield hand against the gate's seam. "Maybe if we-"

The huge statue suddenly came to life, and stood, causing Lessa to shout in alarm.

Uh oh. Rob whirled around to see the statue turn towards him, raising both fists high over its featureless head.

In the next instant, Rob rolled to one side just as the fists crashed into the ground where he'd been. The impact sent large chunks of stone flying everywhere.

Rob had barely managed to stand, again, before the statue swept an arm in his direction. The thing was so fast, he didn't have a chance to react.

He raised his shield just as its forearm crashed into him, and the world went black.

He came to, and found himself a surprising distance away from the statue. His ears were ringing and he had trouble understanding what had happened.

Lessa was shouting, and firing a rapid volley at the statue, which was walking toward him. Its footfalls shook the ground.

Rob spotted a sword a short distance away, and realized it was his. He tried to stand, but his sense of balance had stopped working. Instead, he crawled, feeling the statue behind him getting closer.

Just as he reached it, something happened; a shout from behind. He looked to find Lessa had used her speed to place herself between him and the statue.

The archer fired continuously at the massive thing, and arrows bristled along its stony body.

Rob suddenly found the sword in his hand. When did that happen? He looked down at himself to see he was drenched in blood and understood his head was severely injured. Casting his Healing spell only barely made things better.

Lessa was still shouting, at him or the statue, he couldn't be sure. But she suddenly paused her shots long enough to carefully aim up at the advancing statue.

Just as the monstrosity was nearly on top of her, she fired, striking its smooth face dead center. Amazingly, a large crack formed and ran across its surface. The statue paused, as if confused.

Lessa turned to shout at him some more, and he finally could hear her, over the cacophony in his head.

"Run!"

Rob stumbled away, back toward the street. But the gate's guardian no longer pursued. It changes its focus to Lessa, the arrow still protruding from its face.

The archer backpedaled, firing all the time, drawing it in another direction away from Rob. Her face was of hard concentration.

Suddenly, she nailed it in the face with another shot.

The thing paused, as if uncertain what to do. Rob cast Sun-Bolt on it, but it didn't react.

The statue pointed at Lessa, and its hand curled into a fist.

"Lessa! Watch it!" Rob shouted. His faculties had almost fully returned to him.

"I know!" she shouted back. "We have to get-." She didn't get a chance to finish.

The statue's fist suddenly detached from its arm and shot across the courtyard, like a missile. It crashed into Lessa at full force with a sickening crunch, sending her flying. Both she and the stone fist landed to skid on the ground for a distance.

Rob shouted something; shocked and enraged.

Without thinking, he summoned Henry and pulled himself atop the horse. He charged to where Lessa's crumpled body lay.

The statue began to walk toward her, too, and would reach her first.

Screaming bloody murder, Rob cast a Sun-Bolt directly at the side of its head, causing it to slow and turn.

It gave him just enough time, and he rode up to Lessa, and quickly dismounted. She was covered in blood, and it didn't look like she was breathing. He had to get her away from there.

But before he could, the statue was upon them both, raising its fists high.

As it began its attack, Rob did the only thing he could think of, and pulled out something from one of his pouches.

You have used: Figurine of the Wolf.

Five large, black wolves suddenly appeared in a line between him and the statue. They instantly attacked just as the fists came down, crushing one.

Rob didn't care. With the guardian distracted, he scooped Lessa up and threw her over Henry's saddle. He quickly mounted and raced away, leaving the sounds of crashing fists and snarling wolves behind him.

CHAPTER EIGHT

Once he reached the street, Rob looked back across the courtyard. The wolves danced around the legs of the guardian, confusing it as it tried to attack. Satisfied it wouldn't come after them for a little while, Rob gently pulled Lessa off Henry, and placed her on the ground. She tried to speak, but couldn't, her mouth was mangled, teeth missing.

He placed a healing potion to her mouth, and helped her drink it. Soon, after three more potions, she was whole, again.

"You nearly died," Rob said, finally quaffing a potion himself, now she was in the clear.

Lessa sat up and chuckled. "I still managed to keep a grip on my bow, even in death." She held it up in triumph.

For several minutes, they watched the fighting in the distance. One by one the wolves were crushed, until none remained. They had served their purpose, but Rob wished he could have kept the figurine. A pack of wolves would've been very helpful in other situations.

With the last wolf dispatched, the guardian turned to look in their direction.

"No way," Lessa said, standing in alarm. "Does it still want us?"

But, instead of walking towards them, it returned to its original spot, knelt on one knee, and placed its fists on the ground. The missing fist had reformed.

Rob sighed. "We'll take the hint that we're not ready to fight our way into the other part of the city."

"Fine by me. You need to learn to stay away from killer statues. That was a repeat performance from before."

Both statues had quick reflexes, and he's been caught off guard by each. Maybe he needed to dump more points into Dexterity and Dodge.

Fully recovered, and Henry dismissed, they continued down the street toward the opposite side of the cavern. The wall on the right snaked back to the street and more stone buildings lined the left.

Occasionally, they spotted engraved on the wall, the same ring symbol the guardian had. As to its meaning, Rob had no idea.

The street curved to the right and began to widen. The buildings on the left suddenly terminated at a new wall, which continued along the street. The section with the towers was behind it.

Unlike the partitioning wall, this one wasn't crowned with spikes. Instead, there was a mound of webbing spilling over from the opposite side.

As they continued, the webbing became higher and deeper, covering the base of the towers.

"I don't like the looks of this," Rob said. It reminded him too much of the Goliath Turantula's nest back in the Annex Marsh.

Unfortunately, his worst fears were confirmed. An open gateway appeared, choked with webbing.

Passing it, they moved to the opposite side of the street, along the partition wall, to keep their distance.

From within the webbing, dark figures moved. Their shapes were the telltale form of giant spiders.

"Wonderful," Lessa said. "Please tell me you don't have a quest to go into those towers."

"I don't have a quest to go into those towers," he said as they hurried away from the gate.

"Oh, good."

"But we'll have to go in there at some point."

Lessa sighed, but didn't complain. She knew what she'd signed up for when she agreed to come.

They followed the turn, until the tower section was behind them. The street then split in two directions. The split on the left gradually descended toward the cavern wall, the other led to some structures which didn't resemble anything they'd encountered, so far.

Rob said, "Left or right?"

"I think I hear water down that way," she said, pointing left.

They went left and quickly reached the end of the cavern. Along its edge ran a wide river, which spilled out from a dark hole in the cavern wall.

The street terminated at a long, stone wharf that extended for over a hundred paces aside the river. Various buildings, perhaps ancient warehouses, surrounded the area.

They gazed in amazement at the port. Did boats used to travel this underground river and dock here?

Lessa went to the port's edge and peered down. The water was deep and crystal clear. She scooped up a handful and drank. "Seems clean. Least now we have a water source."

Rob was intrigued by the river. Where did it come from, and where did it go? Another city? He shook his head, telling himself he needed to focus on one ancient, dead city at a time.

They walked back up the street to the split, and took the other direction.

More of the warehouse sized buildings lined this section, and soon it led to another huge open area.

It was like a basketball court, but mammoth in scale. Easily two hundred paces wide, and maybe a thousand long. The partitioning wall lined the opposite side, with the roofs of buildings poking over the top.

They both stopped, surprised and amazed at the scale of this vast space.

"Oh, wow. Look at that," Lessa pointed to the distant, opposite end of the courtyard, which terminated at the cavern wall.

A huge symbol of a ring with clasped hands at its top was carved into the wall. It must have been a couple hundred feet in diameter.

Below it, at ground level, was a large, framed door. Perhaps another gateway like they'd used to enter the cavern?

Rob shook his head in amazement. The scale of the place was truly mind boggling. But what purpose did it serve?

"We should go check it out," Rob said, nodding toward the door.

Suddenly, the cavern grew visibly darker. The brightness dimmed by degrees, as if someone, or something, dialed down all the glowing crystals and fungi at the same time.

In seconds, it was about a third as bright as it had been. Not quite pitch black, but dark enough for them both to cast Light.

They waited with bated breath for several seconds, expecting something to happen.

"What, by the Many-Hells, is happening?" Lessa said, looking around in alarm.

Then Rob realized it. "It's night time. Back above. Night has fallen, and so this place reacts in kind." Amazing. It made sense. Whoever built this place knew it couldn't be perpetual daytime here, deep underground. There needed to be a day and night cycle.

"Okay, now what?" Lessa said. "Light spell or not, I don't want to be running around this place when it's like this."

"We'll head back to the main street and pick a building to make camp in. It's been a long day."

Tired, the two left the massive courtyard behind them, but the mystery of its giant symbol was heavy in their minds.

CHAPTER NINE

Night passed without event.

They'd chosen one of the empty houses midway between the tower section and the guardian's courtyard. It had an intact roof, and, most importantly, a second entrance at the back. They slept on bedrolls stored in Henry's saddlebags, and ate dried fish with bread. Rob took the first four hour shift, sitting in the front doorway to keep watch on the street. He noted the eerie silence which permeated the still air. The place had a creep factor he'd never encountered before. Only the rasp of Lessa's breathing as she slept could be heard, her bow and arrow still in hand.

When it came time to wake her, the archer reacted instinctively, and had a bead on him before her eyes had fully opened.

"Sorry," she said with a sheepish grin.

"No need to apologize," Rob said. Being a light sleeper in this place could be a life saving advantage.

When Rob finally fell asleep, he dreamt of Hope's walls burning, and screaming townsfolk. He was paralyzed, standing helplessly by and watched as his kingdom was destroyed.

He woke with a start, to find Lessa standing over him, looking concerned.

"You okay?" she said.

Rob sat up and looked around. He could still almost smell the smoke from his dream. "Yeah, I'm fine."

"You were tossing and turning all night. When you started shouting, just now, I had to wake you up."

"I was shouting?" Rob stood, feeling a little embarrassed.

"Yeah, something about fire," she said, then looked around. "It must be morning because the light has returned."

Rob went to the doorway. It was bright in the cavern, again, and the street was still and quiet.

He rubbed his beard. What the heck was that dream about? He'd been constantly worried for Hope, and the wall's completion. The stress of which had permeated his dreams.

"What's the plan for the day, boss?" Lessa asked as they ate a breakfast of more bread and dried fish.

Rob swallowed a bite. "I want to inspect that door in the courtyard. Then we can start checking through these houses."

"Checking for what?"

"What else? Loot," he said with a grin.

Breaking camp, they made their way back to the massive courtyard, passing both the gate guardian, and spider towers, without event.

Once they reached the courtyard, Rob summoned Henry, and rode to the door, Lessa running alongside. The colossal ring symbol grew larger and larger with their approach.

They found the door wasn't really a door, at all, but a huge block of smooth stone. It appeared to have been shoved into the doorway, and even extended out a few inches.

The frame around it was lined with small ring symbols, identical to the giant one above them.

Rob searched for some kind of keyhole or mechanism to move the block, but couldn't find one.

"Someone really didn't want anyone to get in there," Lessa said.

Rob pushed at the stone for the millionth time. "I wonder if the builders could cut through this?"

"Could be worth a try. Better than smacking at it with a pick."

"If it comes to that, I'll bring an entire team down here. There has to be something important behind this, or else why go through such an effort to seal it off?"

Disappointed, they made their way back to the building they'd used as camp. Rob decided it made as good a starting point as any.

They entered and searched the building next to it, and found nothing. Then they went to the next building, then the next. Each was barren and nearly empty, save for dust and piles of rocks.

Rob began to feel like this was going to be a complete waste of time, until the tenth building. Near the back, under a stone block, he found something.

Small Diamond.

Value: 25 Gold Pieces.

Encouraged, again, they kept searching. After a dozen more buildings they found another item.

Crystal Goblet.

Value: 50 Gold Pieces.

"This is more like it," Lessa said, holding the goblet up to sparkle in the light.

And so they kept searching. Hour after hour, building after building. Whenever they kept coming up empty handed, they'd find a small treasure. Sometimes they found coins, mostly silver but gold as well. They started to find so much, Henry needed to be summoned so his saddlebags could be used to store it all.

But it all wasn't just treasure they found. Several times they came across mutant ants scouting around. Their numbers weren't great, so a few arrows and a Sun-Bolt, or two, took care of things.

Twice, they came across a giant cave grub, and Rob deemed them too dangerous to deal with. There were ample amounts of other buildings to search than risk fighting something that shot acid.

Eventually, night fell, catching them by surprise.

"The day felt like it went by quickly," Lessa said, slipping a small ruby into Henry's saddlebag.

Rob said, "I'm not going to complain. We've gotten a good haul here. And we have all the other buildings to go through, too."

The money and treasure they found was very encouraging. All of it would go towards Anika's meager coffers. But he would need more. A lot more.

They returned to the first building, dubbing it their base, and made camp.

But shortly after dismissing Henry, Rob was surprised by a sound overhead. A flapping noise.

"What the hell?" he said, quickly drawing his sword and backing into the doorway.

"What? What is it?" Lessa had her bow at the ready.

They listened for a long while, but didn't hear it again.

"It was wings," Lessa said. "I'm sure of it. A dragon?"

"No, not a dragon. Whatever it was had been large, but not dragon sized." But the flapping sound had been vaguely familiar. Could a species of smaller dragon be in the cavern? Anything was possible.

Eventually, when it seemed certain whatever it had been was gone, they made camp, ate, and settled into sleeping shifts. Their entire waking moment was spent on their guard, listening for flapping wings. But the sound didn't return.

The next day was an exact repeat of the previous; searching buildings, finding small items of treasure and coins.

Rob couldn't help but notice the boring sameness of the buildings. Blocks and blocks of them. It was if someone made a copy of a section of buildings and pasted it into the game's program over and over. Lazy. Sort of like the lazy quest titles he'd been getting.

But that was a small quibble. At no point, throughout their explorations, did they stumble across anything which may be deemed an exploit. Rob doubted, whatever it was, the thing would be in one of these copy/paste buildings.

It was either in the Garden within the dome or in the partitioned half of the city. The spider towers were also a possibility.

There were no other places he was aware of that could be a point of interest for this exploit.

That evening, after the light had dimmed and they were settling down for dinner inside their camp building, the sound of flapping wings came. They both jumped to their feet, weapons at the ready.

"It's here," Lessa said, listening. "It didn't fly away."

They each watched a doorway, tensed up and ready for an attack.

After a few moments, Rob grew impatient and called out, "Hello?"

"What are you doing?" Lessa hissed.

"It's not like we need to be quiet. It knows we're here." He went to the front doorway and peered out. Nothing was outside within their Light spell's radius, nor beyond in the gloom of the street.

"Screw it. Follow me," Rob said and cautiously stepped outside.

They scanned about, ready for an ambush, but none came.

"There is definitely something here," Lessa whispered. "I can feel it. Like we're being watched." She turned her head to look up, then shouted. "There! On the roof!"

Rob looked up, and gasped.

The ugliest being gazed down at them. It was humanoid in form, with large gray wings, hunched over with clawed hands gripping the edge of the roof. It had a long, hooked nose and protruding chin. But its most prominent feature were its eyes; red and smoldering with naked hunger.

Rob looked at its name.

Cavern Gargoyle.

Stunned at the hideousness of the new arrival, the two humans could only stare in shock and revulsion. And it glared in return.

Rob sensed this thing was dangerous. It had decided, after checking them out the previous night, that he and Lessa were potential easy pickings. The gargoyle didn't fly away upon being seen.

Then, as if tired with the staring game, the gargoyle stood up, stretching out its immense wings and shrieked at them.

Lessa shot arrows, and Rob cast Sun-Bolt.

Alarmingly, the arrows bounced off its skin, and the Sun-Bolt only seemed to annoy it.

The creature leaned forward and shrieked, again. Only this time, a red wave emanated from its mouth, like a sonic blast.

Both Rob and Lessa suddenly fell backwards to the ground, as if the sound had physically assaulted them.

Rob found he couldn't move or speak.

You have been Mesmerized. You are Stunned. You are Paralyzed.

Oh, damn, was all he could think as he desperately tried to move, but couldn't. There weren't any timers appearing in his vision, telling him how long the effects would last, either.

The gargoyle leapt down from the roof, and landed next to Lessa with ease. It crouched down over her, and sniffed deeply. The creature snorted, and pulled away, uninterested.

It hopped over to Rob, and sniffed his body.

Rob tried with every fiber of his being, to move, and was surprised he could wiggle his legs, but it felt like they were being controlled by someone else. He suddenly felt a genuine fear for his life, and Lessa's.

"You do not belong here, man-thing," the gargoyle said.

Surprised it could speak, Rob struggled to respond but couldn't, only managing a gurgling from his throat.

"You think to take what is not yours," it said. Its voice was like cinder blocks rubbing together.

"We-," Rob managed to sputter, but could say no more. The spell on him was powerful.

"There is no we," the gargoyle said, red eyes glowing. "There is only stone. Silent and eternal. You have woken us. Yes. A mistake you shall learn. Sleep, we were, but no longer."

From the corner of his eye, Rob noticed Lessa shift her arms. She appeared to be regaining some control of her body.

The gargoyle looked at her.

Rob sputtered, "Who are you?" He needed to keep it distracted, no matter how difficult it was.

The monstrosity looked back down at him. "Who? We are of the stone. Once guardians of the Great Circle, but no more. With the Circle broken, those who made us left. Now we sleep and wait for their return. Eons of slumber." Its gaze intensified. "You woke us. You are not natural to the cavern. You must be destroyed."

Lessa had managed to lay the bow on her chest, and was slowly pulling back an arrow. Sweat streamed from her face with the effort.

Rob needed to keep it focussed on him for a few more moments. "Circle? The Great Circle?"

The gargoyle chuckled, which sounded like rocks tumbling down a hill. "You went to its place. We saw you. But it is sealed to only those who are blessed with the knowledge to use it. Still, it is broken. Such knowledge is wasted."

Rob suddenly realized he could move his sword arm, and tightened his grip on it. The creature was too absorbed in its speech to realize the Mesmerizing effects were wearing off.

It leaned closer. "No Circle, no knowledge, no man-things. When you are destroyed, we can sleep again."

"We're not going anywhere," Rob said, and opened the palm of his shield hand.

With the being so close, it was impossible to miss. The Sun-Bolt struck it in both eyes, sending it staggering back, covering its face and shrieking.

An arrow *thunked* directly into its pointed ear, burying deep.

Rob pushed himself up, barely managing a crouch with his body still affected by the gargoyle's spell.

Stunned and in agony, the gargoyle stumbled back, and flapped its wings once.

"Oh, no you don't," Rob said, and lunged forward with a Shield-Bash.

The collision sent the gargoyle smashing through the building's wall. Rob and Lessa pursued.

It was against the far wall, crumpled into a ball with wings sticking out like discarded wrapping paper.

"Must protect the Great Circle," it said, as it tried to stand.

Out of mana for another Sun-Bolt, Rob leapt forward, bringing his sword down upon it with a swing.

Sparks flew as the blade cut through its neck, sending its head tumbling.

The body flailed about, then went still.

The detached head landed on its side, facing them.

"Great Circle-," it said, then the glowing red from its eyes went dark.

Suddenly, the body and head crumbled into piles of broken stone.

The two of them stared at the piles for several moments, then Lessa broke the silence.

"Well, looks like it's time for a new base camp."

CHAPTER TEN

They moved into the building next door, the first one they'd searched, and made camp.

The gargoyle had dropped a Medium Shard of Stone magic.

"This is our key out of here," Rob said.

"Good, because I'm getting a little worried this place would become our permanent residence," Lessa said as she spread out her bedroll. "Did you want to go back to town?"

"No, we're not leaving just yet," Rob said. "We really haven't found anything aside from a little treasure and a lot of dust." And no exploit.

Lessa sighed. "Ants and spiders, then?"

Rob chuckled. "I'll let you choose which one we'll tackle first."

"Oh, wonderful."

The next morning, to his surprise, she chose the ant nest. When he asked why, she shrugged.

"The more we kill of them now, the less we have to deal with later."

When they arrived at the huge dome, and looked down at the streaming columns of mutant ants, her logic made sense. There was no way they could kill everything in one go, there were just too many and they could be swarmed.

For several minutes, they watched the throng go about their business. Their number was intimidating.

"We could go for the queen. Attack it from above, where you saw it from," Lessa said.

"No. It doesn't summon them instantly, only lays eggs which have to hatch. Besides, the moment we attack it, the entire nest would react. We'd still need to reduce their number."

The plan they'd formulated the night before felt foolish now, looking at the mass of insects. But they couldn't come up with another approach which wouldn't get them killed.

Rob placed Henry back on the street, ready for the inevitable retreat, while he and Lessa got close to one of the outlying columns.

Lessa, now at the ready, looked to Rob.

"Let's do it," he said, and readied himself.

She shot the closest ant in the head, killing it instantly. Rob noted he received a portion of the kill's experience points.

When the other ants marching by didn't react immediately, she killed another, then another.

Ants walking over the corpses stopped, antenni quivering as they investigated.

Rob killed an ant which had wandered close with his sword.

More ants stopped to inspect their dead friends. The message of their deaths was being sent back down the scent trail.

"Here we go," Rob said, killing another. Then he summoned both Shale-Mites and sent them on the attack.

Suddenly, the cluster of ants near them all changed directions as one, and surged toward them.

The two adventurers reacted in kind, shooting arrows and swinging swords. Ants died en masse, but never once did any try to escape, they'd been given a signal they had to obey: kill the invaders.

After several minutes, the humans started to back up the wide staircase, Rob at the front, Lessa further behind. The number of ants grew more and more.

Slowly, they ascended backwards on the stairs, killing with a steady rhythm and ant corpses piled in their wake. Hundreds of ants were slaughtered. But at no point did Rob feel they were about to be overwhelmed. Keeping the fighting out in the open, with the advantage of height, made all the difference.

They killed and climbed for what seemed like forever, but soon Rob started to get tired. Even Lessa was showing signs of strain.

Then, just as they reached the top step, Lessa shouted to him. "Almost out of arrows!"

That was their cue.

"Okay, go!"

Turning their backs to the living mass of clicking, snapping ants, they ran back to the street.

A pair of ants had stumbled across Henry, who was trying to defend himself with kicks.

Lessa shot one, and Rob bolted the other.

He leapt atop his mount, and he and Lessa raced down the street.

Behind them, the mutant ants swarmed over everything.

Only when they reached the intersection did they stop and look back.

Ants covered the buildings at the far end of the cavern, searching for them.

"We kicked the mother of all ant nests," Lessa said. She sat on a stone bench and drank from her waterskin.

Rob nodded. "Now we wait and see what happens."

It took the better part of an hour before the throng of ants calmed down, and another hour for them to all return to the nest.

Which suited Rob just fine. The two needed time to rest, and for Lessa's quiver to regenerate.

"How many do you think we killed? Hundreds?" Lessa said.

"Easily. Enough to get me close to hitting level eight." That made for a lot of dead ants.

Lessa checked her quiver, then stood and stretched. "Well, let's go get you to your next level then."

They returned to the dome, to their original spot.

Ants were busying themselves with collecting corpses of their companions and piling them against the cavern wall.

Rob and Lessa killed the workers in their way as they got into position.

The archer looked at Rob. "Ready?"

"Ready."

She fired.

And so it went, killing ants while slowly backing up. The ants reacted the same as before, mindlessly surging forward only to be killed.

Once the two reached the street, they fled as before.

"I think we got more that time. Their numbers are definitely thinning."

"And I hit level eight," Rob said with a wide grin. Despite losing both Shale-Mites in the fray, he felt giddy.

"Gratz!"

For his three attribute points, he put two into Dexterity and one into Strength. As for skill points, he dumped all five into Dodge, bringing it up to 15%.

As they waited for Lessa's quiver to regenerate, Rob noticed the symbol of the ring carved into the side of a pedestal. The Great Circle. This was what the gargoyle had most likely been referring to. It said its purpose was to guard it. Did it mean the giant symbol in the courtyard, or the city in general?

"I think that is the focus point," Lessa said as she worked on replacing the string on her bow.

"Focus point? What do you mean?" Rob ran his fingers around the carving.

"It's said every dungeon has a point for existing. You know, a specific treasure, a weapon of the Gods, a unique spell. Something that is the main reason to delve into the dungeon. I believe it's whatever is under that huge carving."

"Could be the Garden in the dome, too." Whatever that was.

"Maybe the garden is just a happy coincidence, a bonus. With what the gargoyle said, and how prominent that symbol is, my bet is there is something very special to be found behind that block."

Rob had thought more or less the same thing. But could whatever it is be related to the exploit? Or maybe the exploit itself?

Satisfied with her amount of arrows, Lessa stood. "Okay, I'm good to go."

"I was thinking of waiting until tomorrow morning to finish them off. We have a little more than an hour before nightfall." Fighting a swarm of giant ants in the dark was a no go.

"Let's kill as much as we can for a bit."

Rob smiled. "What's made you so eager? You hate those things."

"It's *because* I hate those things. We're close to fully exterminating the bastards. The more we kill tonight..."

"The less we need to kill tomorrow," Rob finished for her.

They returned to the dome, anxious for a fight. But, to their amazement, hardly any ants were around. What few there guarded the entrances.

Rob assessed the new situation. "She's protecting herself."

"The queen?" Lessa fired a hail-mary shot at the distant ants, but missed, striking the ground close by. The ants flinched, but didn't come out to investigate.

"Yeah," Rob said, rubbing his beard. "She knows her numbers have been greatly reduced and she's keeping what she has left."

"So what do we do now? Fight our way in?"

"No, there are still too many. But we could hang back and pick them off. At least until you run out of arrows."

They moved a little closer and Lessa started to shoot at the ants, striking and killing them. Rob stood a little bit ahead of her, ready for a surge. But, amazingly, none came.

One by one the ants were killed. As each died, the others nearby reacted with a flinch, but didn't venture beyond the immediate area of the entranceway. When all the ones Lessa could reach were eliminated, the two shifted to another entrance and repeated the process. Then, something happened.

There were five entryways in all, and had started to pick off the ones at the third entrance, when the ants suddenly ran back into the dome and completely out of view.

"That's it," Lessa said. "She pulled them inside."

Although he's originally planned to finish the nest off in the morning, he felt the impulsive urge to attempt it right then.

But, as if on cue, the cavern started to grow dark.

They returned to their base building to camp for the night.

Lessa was worried about another gargoyle attack, but Rob doubted there were others. Had there been, he suspected they would have attacked as a group. But they were still in their guard for the sound of wings.

When it was his turn to sleep, Rob, again, dreamt of Hope on fire with faceless beings attacking his townsfolk.

CHAPTER ELEVEN

The next morning, after finishing breakfast, Lessa went down to the port to refill their waterskins. Rob sensed she wanted some time to herself and let her go alone. Since leaving Hope several days before, they had spent every second together and neither had any moment of privacy. A break from each other was warranted.

Rob took that time to clean up the camp, and put their things into Henry's saddlebags.

As he puttered about, a message suddenly appeared.

The Log Wall around the town of Hope has been completed.

He laughed at the pleasant surprise. They'd done it! They finished the damn wall!

Rob felt a tremendous sense of relief, like a huge weight had been lifted off his conscience.

Curious, he sat down and pulled out his map book, which opened to his location in the dead city. He flipped to the page showing Anika's valley, and scrolled over to show Hope. The completed line of the wall fully encircled the town. Even the gates could be seen.

Fantastic!

Now the workforce assigned to the wall could be dispersed and redistributed as needed. Rob had left instructions for Saif on how many people should be assigned to various tasks, which were many.

Building the wall had become such a drain on his Kingdom's resources, especially manpower, Rob began to second guess himself. He'd even considered pausing, or greatly reducing, the building effort.

But no more.

Another message appeared.

A Simple Sewage System has been started in the town of Hope.

Rob laughed, again. This time he laughed until tears streamed down his face. It figured Saif would get his sewage project going first. Not that he could be blamed. But it struck Rob as the funniest thing, for some reason. Maybe he had been more stressed over the wall than he realized.

Just then, he heard rapid footfalls out in the street.

Alarmed, he drew his sword and looked out the doorway.

Lessa was racing up the street, a look of concern on her face.

Uh oh, Rob thought.

She arrived, panting heavily.

"There are Gnolls here!" she managed between breaths.

"Gnolls? Where?"

"Down at the port."

"How many?" Rob said, concerned. His good celebratory feelings had been quickly dashed.

"A whole damn army of them!"

"Show me."

They hurried down the street past the spider towers. When they reached the split leading to the port, Lessa stopped. "If we keep going, we'll be seen.

Rob pointed at the large warehouse buildings. "We'll cut through these."

Carefully, the two made their way between the huge buildings, in the direction of the port.

Lessa had told him she had just turned the corner on the street, when a large boat sailed by her view. She immediately hid, just as two more sailed past, each looked to be crammed full of gnolls with black fur. All appeared to be heavily armed.

Rob was surprised by the sudden arrival of other beings in the cavern. He thought the place to be essentially his to explore at his leisure, but that delusion had been shattered.

They picked their way through the buildings, each essentially a huge warehouse comprising a large, single space. Some had smaller rooms, but they ignored them. Exploration would have to wait for another time.

Eventually, they reached a building which sat next to the port. A high ledge with a window offered them a vantage point to look, unseen.

When Rob peeked down, his eyes widened. There were gnolls, alright. Lots of them. They gathered on the stone wharf and appeared to be organizing themselves. They had pitch black fur, and wore a mix of heavy leather armor, or chainmail. Their weapons varied from long spears, to double-edged axes, to swords and bows.

As they watched, two more longboats appeared from the river tunnel, and moored to unload their gnoll passengers.

These gnolls looked a lot tougher than the ones he'd encountered in the Annex Marsh.

By Rob's count, there were a hundred of them, at least.

"What the hell," Rob said. "Why are they here?"

"To make our lives more complicated," Lessa said.

Rob shook his head in confusion. Why bring an army to an empty city which offered only dust and rocks?

"Look," Lessa said, pointing.

Two figures disembarked from one of the newer boats, and stepped onto the wharf. They distinctly stood out from the furry throng around them.

"Humans," Rob said, intrigued.

The two humans, one male, one female, weren't wearing armor or even armed. They wore simple garb, although expensive looking. The man carried a long staff, and the woman had a large, leather bound book in the crook of her arm. From their manner, and the way the gnolls seemed to be giving them space, it looked like they were in charge.

As if to confirm the suspicion, the man started barking orders at the gnolls, who reacted in kind.

In moments, the gnolls formed into a long column, four abreast. Then the man shouted something and the entire column started marching in perfect lockstep.

Rob watched the small army march down the length of the wharf and exit the port, out of sight.

"Where are they going?" Lessa said, worry etched on her face.

"I think I know," Rob said. "Come on."

They followed the column as it moved through the wide streets of the warehouse district. It wasn't hard as their footfalls made them easy to locate.

Rob and Lessa stayed back about a block, just in case, but at no time did the gnolls scout the surroundings. In fact, they didn't make any effort to see if anyone else was around.

For several minutes the gnolls marched, and it soon became clear exactly what their destination was.

They marched out onto the vast courtyard and turned toward the symbol of the Great Circle. Their feet kicked up a thin cloud of dust behind them.

Rob and Lessa watched from a rooftop as the gnolls reached the far wall. Then, the column broke up and a great amount of activity took place.

"Can you make out what they're doing?" Rob said.

Lessa squinted. "It looks like they're setting up camp."

Tents began to sprout up, and even campfires were made.

"Looks like they intend to stay awhile," Rob said, shaking his head. "My guess is they intend to gain access to whatever is behind that stone block."

"I can see the man and woman at the doorway, looking at it. Should we go in for a closer look?"

"No, too risky. See, they're finally setting up guards in the nearby structures."

A dozen or so gnolls sauntered away from the camp and entered the nearest buildings.

"What now?" Lessa said, frustrated. "This really throws a dungball into our plans. How can we get anything done with those dog-men running around?"

"Let's just wait and watch them for a while, see if anything happens."

Several hours passed, but, other than regular camp activities, nothing interesting occurred. The two humans eventually went into one of the bigger tents, and didn't reemerge.

Eventually, Rob reached a decision. "This doesn't change our immediate plans of finishing off the ant queen."

"Because they don't seem to care about anything other than that doorway?"

"Yeah. They haven't even sent out patrols. It's like they know the place. Maybe they're been here before. They certainly knew where the blocked doorway was located."

"So we go back to our slaughter, and hope we don't get discovered."

"They won't hear us way the hell on the other side of the city. I think it's worth the risk. What about you?"

Lessa grinned. "Sounds exciting."

CHAPTER TWELVE

They left their hiding place by the courtyard, and the gnoll army, and returned to the huge dome. The entire time, they were on their toes, half expecting a warparty of gnolls to fall upon them. But none did. They didn't see any gnoll scouts, nor encounter a patrol.

Rob had written off the spider towers. That section was too close to the port, and any fighting there would be detected. But he would return to them once it was safer. There had to be loot inside and he wanted it.

At the dome, they found the five entryways unguarded. Not a single ant could be seen anywhere.

"They're all inside, with the queen," Rob said.

"Let's do this," Lessa said.

For the next hour, they cleared out all the entryways of ants, which had pulled farther back into the dome. One by one, the tunnels were purged. Each time, Rob pulled them back outside when they got in too far.

At the deepest part of the last tunnel, the queen's chamber could be seen. Clearly agitated, she hunched atop her mound, quivoring and snapping her colossal mandibles.

Several dozen giant ants were between her and the human invaders. These were all she had left.

"Pick 'em off," Rob said.

From the relative safety of the tunnel, Lessa fired at the remaining ants. A group rushed toward them, and Rob hit one with a Sun-Bolt and slew the rest.

As if sensing this was the end-game, the queen commanded the last of her brood to attack.

Which was exactly what Rob wanted.

When the ants swarmed forward, he and Lessa immediately backed up, firing and slashing. The last ant died to an arrow, about midway down the tunnel.

Lessa laughed and they returned to the queen's chamber.

The huge insect snapped its mandibles and hisses at them.

"Ah, shut up!" Lessa said, and hit the queen's head with an arrow.

The queen's hissing intensified, and a sudden gush of liquid spewed out from its mouth.

"Watch out!" Rob said, shoving Lessa aside and sending her flying with his great strength.

The liquid splattered to the ground and bubbled, eating away at the stone.

Before they could do anything, the queen spit another arc of acid, causing them to retreat into the tunnel.

Safely out of range, they watched as she spat acid at the tunnel entrance, over and over.

"How much does she have of that stuff?" Lessa said.

Rob looked at the growing lake of acid, and considered going through one of the other tunnels, but thought better of it. "Come on."

They went back outside, and climbed up the side stairway Rob had used before. Once at the top, Rob sheathed his sword and fished out a pair of sharded stones.

He counted to three, and they quickly stood, with Lessa shooting at the exposed queen below.

Surprised, the gigantic ant attempted to turn its vast bulk, and tilt its head up at them.

But Rob didn't give the monster a chance, and used both stones at once.

You have cast Lightning.
You have cast Lightning.

Twin bolts of lightning arced down from the dome's roof, and ripped through the queen's body. The huge insect shuddered and collapsed, all the while Lessa kept piercing it with arrows. Within moments, it died.

Quest complete: Pest Control.

You have cleared the dome of all the ants, and their queen.

Reward: 5,000 Experience Points.

"Finally," Lessa said. "That was quite the light show."

"A light show inside. I don't think I could have done that outside, without attracting attention. Let's go see what loot she dropped."

It took several minutes to search around the queen's corpse, with pools of acid and guts everywhere, but Rob found a little pile of items under a giant, severed antenna.

You have taken an item: 2 x Medium Shard of Life magic.

You have taken an item: Mobile Ant Mound.

You have taken an item: Ant Mount Bracelet.

There was also a money bag filled with a thousand gold pieces.

Rob took a closer look at the two ant items, the first, a stone carved in the shape of a fist-sized ant.

Figurine of Mobile Ant Mound.

Creates a stationary mound from which 30 - 50 Mutant Ants would emerge to fight within, or defend, an area.

Duration: 3 hours.

Can be used once every 24 hours.

He whistled. Another summonable ally. That was a great item.

The second was a bracelet created from a chain of interlocking ants, biting into each other.

Ant Mount Bracelet.

Summons a large mutant ant which could be ridden.

60 minute respawn timer if killed.

"This one's for you," Rob said, handing Lessa the bracelet.

Her eyes grew wide as she examined it. "Finally! My own mount!" She put it on, then summoned it.

A huge mutant ant appeared beside them. It was physically identical to the many they'd killed, but was easily several times larger. Its saddled back came up to Lessa's chest.

With a laugh of delight, she jumped onto it, slipping her boots into the stirrups and grabbing its reins.

"How do I look?"

"Ridiculous!" Rob laughed. "But it beats using up your running ability."

"Oh, I can make it attack, too. Look." She pulled at the reins a certain way and the ant nashed its large, serrated mandibles together.

With one final check around for any other items, Rob turned his attention to what the true purpose of destroying the nest was for.

They approached the back where the small entryway was located.

Peering inside revealed a small chamber. Glowing crystals covered every surface within. It was bright enough to make the two squint against the harsh light.

Cautiously, Rob stepped inside, while Lessa watched from the entrance.

Rob felt an immediate spike in the temperature as he carefully stepped across the crystal covered floor.

In the middle of the chamber was a large mound of crystals, arranged into a rectangle, like an altar.

"What the hell is this place?" Rob said, amazed at the various twinkling colors.

"Try touching it," Lessa said, indicating the altar.

"Thanks for volunteering me," Rob said. "Why don't you?"

"Sorry. Someone has to stay out here and look after their new mount."

With a sigh, Rob touched his gloved hand on the glowing altar.

A message appeared.

You have discovered a Shard Garden!

Insert shards within the crystal bed to create more shards.

Rob felt himself go numb with surprise. "Well, I'll be damned!"

CHAPTER THIRTEEN

"What is it? What's to be damned over," Lessa said.

Rob said, "Hang on a second. I need clarification here." He took out one of the Medium Shards of Life magic and held it over the altar. "What do I do now?"

"How should I know?"

"Not you." He was speaking to the game.

A message appeared.

Insert a shard into a socket within the crystal bed. Over time, the shard will grow in size; minor to medium, medium to major. Once the shard is major, it will create 1 - 3 minor shards of its type, which will also grow. The more major shards of a specific type in the garden, the faster the growth rate becomes for that type.

"Holy cow," Rob said, still stunned. This was amazing. If it worked.

He inserted the end of the medium shard into a crystalized socket, which was the same shape, and it clicked into place. The crystal bed around it began to glow brighter. Then, the shard itself started to glow.

Rob watched in anticipation for several minutes, but nothing else happened. A shard didn't appear to be growing.

"How long will it take for this shard to grow into a large one?"

He waited for an answer, but none came.

Curious, he inserted the second Medium Shard of Life magic next to the first and it brightened.

"Maybe it's broken," Lessa suggested, helpfully.

"It's not broken. It obviously takes time, but I should be able to know how long." Unless the answer was being withheld from him, which wouldn't be a surprise.

Annoyed, he said, "I want to know how long a medium shard takes to grow into a major one."

To his surprise, another message appeared, but it was not what he expected.

Output Error.

Time variable for item not defined.

Error # 7775-342.

Reference Shard module F7a.

"Whoa," Rob said, stunned at what he was reading. This wasn't an answer, and he didn't think it was meant to be seen. It had something to do with the programming of the game.

He laughed. If ever there was an example needed to prove he was in a simulation, this was it.

He asked, again, about the shard's growth rate.

This time, no error message appeared. Nor did any other.

Rob laughed. He envisioned geeky men in lab coats scrambling around and looking into giant manuals. The thought was incredibly cathartic.

"My guess is days," Lessa said. "For things as valuable as shards, it would be expected to take a while."

He had to agree, but he couldn't help but smirk in satisfaction at what he stumbled upon. It proved to him something more valuable than anything else: the creators of this game weren't infallible.

Knowing he was being watched at that very moment, Rob shrugged and strolled out of the chamber. "Guess whoever put this garden here didn't know what they were doing. Maybe they should be fired."

Lessa looked at him like he was nuts.

Outside the chamber, Rob took out a sharded stone of Stone Barrier Unger had given him, and slapped it next to the entrance. In moments, stone grew over the opening, completely sealing it off.

"Hopefully this will keep the gnolls from finding it," he said. "I think it's time for us to go home. What about you?"

"I'm all for it. I can show off my new mount to everyone," she said, petting the ant's hard exoskeleton.

They left the dome, passing many crumpled ant corpses. Climbing the stairs to the street revealed the ant's footfalls, although not as loud as Henry's, were still a little too loud for their liking, so Lessa dismissed it.

"What are you going to name it?" Rob said as they reached the street.

"I dunno. Mount, I guess."

"Mount? That's not a name."

"It's what the thing is. How about Ant?"

Rob sighed.

"Or Anty. Hey, I like that. Anty it is."

Rob didn't really care what she called the thing. His mind kept playing over the error message, and the chaos it must be causing back in the real world, at that very moment. God, how he wished he could see that!

Just before reaching the intersection, Lessa suddenly held up a fist and they stopped. Listening intently for a moment, she then grabbed Rob by the arm and they quickly ran into the closest, ruined building.

Once inside, Lessa held a finger to her lips. They sat in the shadows and listened.

After several moments, Rob heard boots marching on stone. Then gnolls appeared on the street, coming from the direction of the giant courtyard. There were about twenty in all, each armed.

The woman was with them, still carrying the book. She held it open in front of her as she walked, reading from it.

The group suddenly stopped in the intersection, much to Rob's alarm. What were they doing here, this far from their camp? Had they detected him and Lessa somehow?

The two held their breath and watched the new arrivals with a mixture of alarm and curiosity.

The woman panned the book around, as if using it to see her surroundings. Her expression of concentration changed to surprise.

She said, "There has been recent activity here. Very recent."

The gnolls tensed and looked around toward the buildings next to the street.

Rob and Lessa ducked back. They looked for a back doorway, but there wasn't one. The only way out was the way they came.

"Scavengers?" one of the gnolls said, its voice gruff.

"Perhaps," said the woman. "It looks like they've passed along the street here several times."

"How many? Can you even tell with that thing?"

"Not an exact number, no," she said, sounding annoyed at the question. "But not many. A small group, perhaps."

How could she tell that? Was the book magical?

The woman sighed. "This only reinforces my suggestion that patrols are implemented, at least during the day."

"His Lordship wants all forces concentrated in the courtyard. He considers the rest of the city irrelevant."

"And leaves us blind to any potential threats," she said, "like whoever has passed through here. I want daytime patrols, sergeant. I will inform his Lordship."

"Yes, your Ladyship." The gnoll then spoke to the others using its own grunting language.

Through the doorway, Rob saw pairs of gnolls move off in different directions.

The woman began to speak again, but suddenly stopped, as if realizing something. "There is something inside that building, right there."

Oh damn. Rob knew she was talking about them. Lessa looked at him in alarm, expecting a signal to attack, but he shook his head.

The timer on his mites had just expired, so he quickly summoned them and sent them flying out the door.

There were shouts of surprise, followed by a flash of light. One of the Shale-Mite's health indicators instantly went to zero and died. The other, he ordered to fly away.

"More giant bugs," he heard the woman say. Had he fooled them?

Just then another gnoll ran up to the group. "Your Ladyship, his Lordship is asking for your immediate presence."

"Of course he does," she said, sounding frustrated. "Let us see what his *Lordship* wants now."

Rob heard the group walk away. After several minutes, he peeked outside and found the street was empty.

"Who was that?" Lessa said.

"I don't know, but she can cast a hefty lightning spell." It appeared to be a stronger version than he used on the ant queen. "I don't intend to find out, at the moment. They're a problem to be dealt with later."

Cautiously, they moved out onto the street, mindful of the gnoll patrols which could spot them. Thankfully, a patrol didn't go in the direction of the entrance.

Rob recalled his remaining mite and the two of them hurried toward the doors, keeping close to the cavern wall. All the while, they expected to be discovered, but they reached them without incident.

With a quick look around, Rob inserted the Stone shard. The huge stone doors groaned open, and they went inside.

They waited for the doors to close for what felt like forever. When the doors finally closed, Rob let out a sigh of relief.

"We could have fought them," Lessa said as they started down the tunnel. "Why didn't we?"

"If we did, we'd end up fighting all of them. I really don't want to start anything with an entire army, right now. There's also no telling if more are coming. They only seem interested in that circle thing for now, and I want to keep it that way." At least until he can figure out how he should deal with them should they decide to go exploring, and come to the surface.

If that happened, he'd have a real problem on his hands.

CHAPTER FOURTEEN

They traveled back up through the tunnel without incident. When they passed the hole overlooking the city, Lessa asked if he wanted a quick look.

"Been there, done that," he said. He'd had his fill of the place, but knew he'd have to return. There was still treasure to be found, and the mystery of the Great Circle to be solved.

And the exploit. He wasn't sure if the error message had anything to do with it, but felt his 'real world ally' would find a way to let him know, regardless.

After several hours, they reached the surface and stepped outside the cave mouth at the base of the tree. It was past midday and sunshine fought to get through the thick canopy overhead.

"Ah, fresh air," Lessa said, breathing deeply. "Time for freshly cooked food and an actual bath."

"Agreed," Rob said. They'd only been roughing it for a few days, but with all the fighting and sweating, they smelled like animals.

Before leaving, Rob used his last Stone Barrier on the cave mouth, sealing it up.

"That won't stop 'em," Lessa said, summoning Anty.

"No, but it will give us a little warning if they try to break through it. I'm going to assign a lookout nearby to watch, just in case. It should give us some warning."

"Do you think they'll even come all the way up here?"

"I hope not, but we need to be ready, either way."

They rode away from the cave and through the swamp. It felt good to be outside again, with the wind and sounds of a living, breathing world around them.

But when they reached the east-west branch in the path, which led to the mines and back to Hope, something was wrong.

Large swathes of trees had been knocked down and even crushed. It was so obvious, a trail of destruction could be seen leading from the area of the swamp and then northward.

Something huge had forced its way through here.

Rob had a chilling realization of what it could be, and swallowed.

Just then, a town's guardsman stumbled out of some nearby underbrush.

"My Lord!" he said, with visible relief. "Thank the Gods you've returned!"

Rob and Lessa dismounted and ran over to the young man, who was bleeding from the mouth and nose.

Rob caught him as he keeled over, and cast Heal on him. "What is it? What happened?"

The guard took a swallow from a Healing potion Lessa held up for him.

"Q-Quartek the Cruel," he managed. "He's out of the swamp."

Rob felt himself grow cold with dread. It was as he feared. The monster had finally left the comfort of its home turf. But why?

"One of the rangers got too close to the swamp," the man said. "I don't know if she antagonized him, or simply came upon him by mistake. But the thing took an immediate dislike to her and gave chase." He motioned at the destruction around them.

"When did this happen," Rob said.

"They just went through here not five minutes ago."

Rob wasn't ready for a fight with that horrific monster. He knew it. But something had to be done. There was no telling how much death and destruction the crocodile would do if it wasn't stopped.

It was at that moment, Rob realized there was only one option.

He stood and removed all his armor, stuffing them in Anty's saddlebags.

"What in the Many-Hells are you doing?" Lessa looked at him like he was mad.

"Something crazy." Rob then removed all his jewelry as well, but his Shalemite didn't despawn when he took off its ring. When finished, he stood in his basic clothes, save for his boots and Henry's bracelet. He then took the guardsman's sword which sheathed across his back.

Curious, he removed Henry's bracelet, and the horse didn't wink out of existence. He placed the bracelet in the saddlebags, then mounted the horse.

"You want to fight an elite monster in your underwear, wielding a basic sword?" Lessa said, aghast.

"Get back to Hope, and prepare a defense. He may try to destroy the town if this doesn't work." He knew how vengeful the creature was.

"If what doesn't work?" Lessa said, but he rode off, following the trail of damage.

Rob rode Henry as fast as the horse could manage, jumping fallen trees, and passing over deep gouges in the ground where the crocodile had landed. He was pleased to notice whoever the ranger Quartek was after, she was leading him away from the central valley.

It didn't take long to find where they were.

As he passed through a clearing, he spotted a massive tail slide over the edge of a hill. Riding up to the spot, he saw Quartek launching itself into a copse of trees, snapping and crushing them. From the other side, a woman darted out and ran for her life at top speed. To Rob's amazement, she ran faster than even Lessa using her ability. He recognized her as the ranger who'd been up in the tree before.

The crocodile thrashed its way out of the copse and looked for its elusive prey.

Rob was already racing directly at Quartek, shouting obscenities. The monster was so focused on the ranger, it didn't notice him. The thing then found the woman and began propelling itself along the ground, using its great belly like a sled.

But Rob managed to get within range and cast Sun-Bolt at the side of its massive head.

The crocodile flinched as the blast struck it by an eye, and whipped its head around. It locked gazes with Rob, and hissed with rage.

Oh, boy, Rob thought, as he pulled Henry around. He'd wanted Quartek's attention, and he got it.

Still sliding, Quartek used its legs to turn and move towards Rob, the ranger completely forgotten.

Rob then went back across the clearing, through the trail of destruction, shale-mite in tow. He needed to get the monster moving south.

Careful not to let his pursuer lose sight of him, Rob had to contend with moving through the forest. For Quartek, trees and boulders were just a nuisance to barrel through. What lead Rob had was quickly evaporating.

When he suddenly found himself crossing the main path, again, he felt some relief. He had his bearings, and altered his direction. There wasn't any need to check if Quartek still followed. The snapping of trees, and its hissing let him know exactly where it was, and it was getting louder. He could almost feel the creature's hatred, like a stifling wave continuously washing over him. Good.

Soon, a mist slowly appeared around him, growing thicker and thicker. His body tingled with anticipation, but there was still a chance Quartek might catch him.

As if on cue, he heard the crocodile suddenly growl. A quick glance back told him what it was about to do.

Having gotten close to its prey, but not as fast as it wanted, the crocodile hopped into the air, putting its massive tail beneath its body. Then, it flicked the tail, launching itself like a missile through the air.

Having seen this tactic before, Rob anticipated it, and yanked on Henry's reins the moment Quartek was airborne, turning them out of its path. Had he not done so at the exact moment, he would have been killed.

The crocodile shot through the air, blocking out the sky and flew past where Rob had been. It tried to bite him, snapping its colossal jaws just above his head, but got his shale-mite instead.

The titanic reptile smashed into the underbrush, sending trees and dirt flying everywhere.

And Rob kept riding. The crocodile recovered quickly, and pursued.

But the thickening mist started to make things harder to see, to the point Rob had to slow down or risk colliding into something.

Quartek was having difficulties, too, but that didn't make it give up the pursuit. Rob could hear it smashing about behind him.

As he tried to figure out where he was at, he felt a momentary sense of panic that he wasn't where he meant to be.

Then he nearly rode at full tilt into a block of stone sitting in the forest. He could see another huge block a short distance away. Was this the place?

He slowed down to navigate through the blocks. They were familiar to him, but not quite the same. He couldn't be sure if he'd messed up directions rushing through the trees.

Suddenly, the sky grew dark and he looked up to find Quartek descending on him.

Rob leaped from the saddle just as the massive crocodile landed. One of its huge forelegs caught Henry. The impact of the croc's body sent the horse tumbling and crashing against a block.

Rob had rolled away, but felt his right arm break when he landed. For a few seconds, he was dazed.

The cries of pain from Henry brought him back to reality. The horse was crumpled in a ball, flailing its legs. Two of them were obviously broken.

As Rob tried to stand, a massive head appeared over the block next to Henry. Quartek looked down upon its helpless prey, drool running from its opening mouth.

But as the creature lunged downward, Rob despawned Henry. Quartek's jaws snapped empty air, hitting the ground.

Rob turned and ran. He heard the crocodile behind, clamoring over the stone blocks.

Was this even the place? Rob navigated through the large blocks, some as big as houses, until the ground started to slope downward. Then, just as he was starting to believe he was truly lost, he saw it.

At the bottom of the slope, across a small clearing, was the tower.

A chill ran through his body the moment it came into view. It looked quite different than before, shaped like an arching tusk of ivory with a glowing window carved near its top.

Along its base was a thick mat of webbing, each strand as thick as his arm. Next to it, from behind a mound of boulders, he could see a pair of long, black legs.

It took only a second or two to take all this in, enough time for Quartek to find him.

Too big to pass between the stone blocks, it climbed along the top of them, getting closer.

Rob ignored his growing fear, and ran down the slope. Without his necklace of speed, he noticed the difference it had made.

As he reached the bottom, and began to race across the clearing, things emerged from the ground around him.

Half expecting the grass covered shamblers from before, he was horrified to see these were worse.

Huge, brown praying mantises pulled themselves up out of the dirt. Each was as tall as him, with long arms covered in chitinous spikes. Their triangular heads turned to track him with huge, insect eyes.

But Rob didn't care about them. His focus was getting to the tower.

Behind him, he heard Quartek slide down the slope, and into the clearing at a high speed. It propelled itself along, knocking mantises aside like toys. The croc only wanted Rob, and it was close to getting him.

Dodging several attacks from the mantis-creatures, Rob reached the other side of the clearing and ran directly at the tower. A door could be made out through the thick mass of webbing covering it.

As Rob reached the outer layer of webbing, he stopped. From behind the mound of boulders, the black legs moved and a gigantic spider partially revealed itself.

Goliath Black Widow (Elite)

Rob felt his bowels liquify in fear as the living nightmare slowly moved out of its hiding place. The terror he felt was completely overwhelming.

But he kept himself from running away, screaming. Instead, fighting the instinct to survive, he turned his back to the spider, and faced Quartek.

The croc propelled itself across the clearing. As it got closer, it used its tail ability, and launched itself like a missile, directly at Rob.

And Rob grinned.

In the moment before Quartek, flying through the air, reached him, two things happened. The croc suddenly noticed the spider, and Rob jumped sideways, out of the way.

As the croc hit the ground at top speed, Rob was smacked by its swinging tail. He hit a boulder and felt bones breaking throughout his body. The world went black and when he opened his eyes again, he found himself surrounded by giant, man-sized mantises descending upon him.

But he didn't care. From between the insects, he saw Quartek lodged in the thick webbing and flailing. As the croc did so, the Goliath Black Widow, which was of comparable size, spun more webbing onto it.

Rob felt the mantises start to slash at him, and he instinctively struck back with his sword. But it didn't matter, he knew what the outcome would be. He'd known the moment he entered the Annex Marsh, he wouldn't be leaving.

At least not alive.

As he received more blows, and lost more blood, he collapsed to the ground, his hit points dropping quickly.

But the last thing he heard was a monstrous cry of agony as the black widow bit the cocooned Quartek.

Then the final darkness claimed him, and he smiled.

You have died.

CHAPTER FIFTEEN

"This is impressive," Rob said. "You two have done an amazing job."

"Thank you," said Trenton, "The carpenter and I make for a good team."

The two men walked along the outer perimeter of the completed wall, allowing Rob to inspect what he'd invested so much time and resources into.

Each log was buried several feet deep into the ground, and wedged so tightly together an ant couldn't crawl between them.

Rob said, "When I received the message it had been finished, I couldn't believe it. I didn't expect it to be done for a few more days." He smacked one of the logs in appraisal.

Trenton shrugged. "We thought it would make a great gift for you, once you returned from that dungeon, which is why we all doubled our efforts."

It had been a full day since Rob died in the Annex Marsh, and resurrected. His plan of removing all his gear had paid off. The death penalty resulted in him only losing the basic sword he'd taken from the ranger. Everything else was waiting for him in Hope, along with Lessa, and a cheering crowd.

He felt elated at getting rid of Quartek, but it was tempered by not actually killing the monster himself. That honor went to the Goliath Black Widow.

He imagined the giant croc, all cocooned and helpless, its innards liquifying for the spider to sup upon at her leisure.

Yet, he still had the quest. When the monster finally died, would he fail it? It didn't matter. The loss of all the experience points he'd gotten from the ant nest was worth ridding the valley of that annoying crocodile.

The two men walked along the wall and reached the eastern gate. Its doors were open inward, and people traveled through, going about their business. Some were workers assigned to wood or iron ore, while others were heading out to forage.

The gate was made of thick wooden planks backed with iron plating. When closed, a long block of wood across a middle bracket kept it locked.

All four gates were made in this manner. Gunther had said an upgrade should be considered, but the current gates should hold against most sieges.

Most sieges. Even with the wall finished, Rob worried about an attack. He suspected it would always be that way, too.

They strolled through the gate and into town. People greeted him and waved. Having spent a few days with only Lessa for company made him appreciate the presence of others.

Trenton said, "Now that the wall is done, should I return to the quarry? We do have quite the stockpile of stone, but it wouldn't hurt to have more."

"I have a project for you," Rob said, and smiled when the builder's eyes lit up.

"Really? What? The inner wall? That will be a hefty project, one which will take a lot of time and, uh, money." He leaned forward, to whisper. "And I can offer a great discount if you don't mention it to the guild."

"No, not the stone wall. That'll have to wait. But I need something almost as important."

"What?"

They arrived at a spot roughly in the middle of town, a few blocks from the western sallyport. A four way intersection was formed by the adjoining streets, and left a large space in the middle.

"A Constabulary," Rob said. He'd scouted out this spot beforehand and knew, with some adjustments, it would offer enough space for one.

Trenton was delighted and watched as Rob moved the nearest homes, one by one. The homeowners had been warned, and didn't voice any objections. Noone wanted to disappoint their king.

After a few minutes, all the homes had been turned or shifted into new positions, making the space of the intersection over twice as large.

Rob pulled up his kingdom menu, and scrolled through the available buildings list. He found the Simple Stone Constabulary, and selected it. The structure's outline appeared, and he set it into place.

It was a squat, two story building made entirely of stone. The ground floor had several rooms including prison cells. The top floor was made up of living quarters for the town's guard. A narrow courtyard surrounded the building closed in by a stone wall, seven feet tall.

The building resembled a minicastle. Which was the point.

Trenton laughed with delight, clapping Rob on the back. "Oh, this is a wonderful project, my Lord. Expensive, but well worth it."

"Can you start right away?"

"You bet I can!" the builder said, then ran off, shouting for workers.

Rob left him to his work and wandered back outside in the direction of the distant treeline.

While he'd been on guard duty, back in the dead city, he'd spent time exploring his kingdom menus. The need for a structure in town, to substitute for the castle, was paramount in his mind. If the walls failed to keep invaders out of the town, a secure building had to be ready. He found the Constabulary building suited that need exactly, as well as serving a general purpose as a police station. After the encounter with the thief it would only be a matter of time before another came to Anika. Prison cells, with iron bars forged by the blacksmith, would give him a place to put them.

He needed to consider other criminals, as well, not just thieves. At some point, someone was going to do something which would require imprisoning them.

Rob crossed the wide field and approached a large wooden warehouse-like structure parked next to the forest. It was Gunther's newly completed woodshop, something the carpenter had been chomping at the bit to make since he'd arrived in Hope. With the wall finished, it had taken him less than a day to construct it.

Inside were several people at worktables, cutting, chopping and shaving various items, mostly furniture. Many of the new arrivals had only brought what they could carry, creating a need for furnishings.

"Where's Gunther?" he asked a worker.

"In the back, my Lord, playing with his new saw."

He found the carpenter shouting at a pair of workers, who were cutting a log using a wide saw. Each had a saw's end and were slicing through the dense wood.

"How is it?" Rob said.

"Oh, it's okay, I guess," Gunther said. "It'll get the job done, slowly. Iron blades work in a pinch, but steel ones are where it's at."

Without steel, Kortz had to make the large saw blade with iron, which wears down quickly and requires more work to keep sharp.

Gunther said, "Cutting logs into usable lumber is labor intensive. If I'm going to keep up with all the demand in town, I'm going to need another blade."

"I'll talk to Kortz about getting you more. How many do you think you need?"

"As many as I can get. There's a lot to cut. But what I also would like is to open a woodshop in Crossroads."

"Why's that?"

"Transporting cut lumber is a pain when the wagons and oxen are at a premium. All the ones in town are spoken for, and Zuthus has the rest. There's plenty of trees to cut down south, and a woodshop would spread the work around."

Rob suspected this was exactly what Zuthus wanted, too. Having the facility to cut lumber would help his little village grow. And Rob couldn't begrudge him for wanting it, either. If he was in the troglodyte's place, he'd want it, too.

"Okay, set up a Crossroad's woodshop," Rob said.

Gunther laughed. "I knew working with you would be a pleasure, my Lord. Now, if you will excuse me, I have an apprentice to send south."

Rob walked north from the woodshop, along the tree line. Jace had set up a small meeting area for the rangers, someplace away from the bustle of town.

He found a large lean-to made of branches and leaves, with benches and a used fire-pit. But no Jace.

Having not used his tracking skill in ages, he considered trying to locate the woodsman as practice. An extra percentage or two added to the skill wouldn't hurt.

But before he started into the forest, a voice close by startled him.

"I thought it would be harder for us to avoid your detection," Jace said, stepping out from behind some trees. A young ranger, a woman, was with him.

"Didn't you hear us?" she asked, and Rob recognized her as the ranger Quartek had chased.

"Not at all," Rob said. "How long have you been hiding there?"

Jace said, "We weren't hiding. He followed you, all the way from the woodshop."

Rob chuckled. "I had no idea." Although it was impressive, it was a stark reminder to have his shale-mites around him on guard duty when outside town. Having the insects flying about while in Hope frightened the people too much. "How goes the recruitment?"

Jace said, "There are now almost two dozen rangers scouting around the valley. We'll need a little more so shifts can be covered, but we'll get that in time."

"Anything to report?"

"Nothing significant. One ranger said he thought saw a goblin northeast, at the edge of the mountains. A female goblin, at that."

A female goblin? He hadn't seen one before. Or killed one, either.

Jace said, "It ran away, and the ranger lost its tracks. Should we try to find and kill it?"

"No, not a priority. I'm more concerned about armies crossing the ranges. And the Watchers of the Range? Are they all in position?"

The big man scratched his red beard. "Fenton has assigned his watchers along the mountains, but there are about half as many watchers as I'd like, to be honest. The position is hard to fill."

"Why is that?"

"You are sitting out in the deep woods, alone, and far from help if it's needed. But that, too, will fill out over time."

The young woman suddenly spoke up. "My Lord, I wanted to take this opportunity to apologize to you." The woman looked crestfallen.

"What for?"

"I didn't intend on bringing Quartek out of the swamps. It was my fault, though. I was too close, ranging between there and the mountains. Even though I kept as far away as possible, the monster appeared and gave chase."

"What's your name?"

"Jillian, my Lord."

"There is nothing to apologize for, Jillian. In fact, it turned out to be a good thing."

"How so?" she asked, looking a little less nervous.

"It presented an opportunity to get rid of that bastard, once and for all. In fact, I want to thank you."

"Thank me?" she said, wide-eyed. "But you died because of me."

Rob shook his head. "No, not because of you. I chose to die as a means to trap Quartek in the marsh. Now we'll never have to worry about him."

Jillian smiled brightly, blushing.

"I noticed you can run incredibly fast," he said.

She nodded. "Yes, an ability blessed upon by the gods at my birth. It's saved my life many times."

Jace then pointed, and said, "A guard is coming."

A young man was racing across the clearing. Behind him, the town suddenly went into a frenzy of activity with shouts of alarm.

Oh, no, Rob thought. What now?

The man ran up, panting. "My Lord! There are goblins at the north gate!"

"Goblins?" Rob said, alarmed. Were they the raiders?

"Yes, my Lord! We're being invaded!"

CHAPTER SIXTEEN

Rob summoned Henry and his mites, and raced back to town. Guards were assembling on the battlements, and people from outside the walls were running through the gates.

Instead of going through town, he chose to circle around and get a look at the enemy from the side. Maybe even flank them.

His heart pounded in his chest. They'd come. He knew they would, eventually, and now they were here.

As he raced around the northeast perimeter of the wall, the north gate came into view. At first, he didn't see anything, no hordes of warriors storming the walls.

He scanned the area, and spotted a small cluster of figures a hundred paces up the road. Almost immediately, he could see they were goblins. But something was different.

When he got closer, he noticed there were only three of them, unarmed and cowering together. One held up a branch with a torn, white cloth on it. As Rob got closer, the goblin with the flag waved it frantically.

"Peace!" shouted the flag bearer. "Don't kill us! We come in peace!"

Rob recognized both the voice, and the goblin. "Hazziq?" he said, riding up to them. "Is that you?"

Hazziq's eyes brightened. "Yes, it is me, mighty king! Your loyal follower and friend. Please, don't let them kill us!"

Rob looked at the gate. Guards packed the opening, and archers lined the battlements above. Saif stood with them, ready to cast his Lightning spell.

After a quick glance over the three new arrivals, to ensure it wasn't some kind of trick, Rob shouted for everyone to stand down.

The tension in the air lessened, but the guards stayed wary.

"I'm surprised to see you here," Rob said. "The last time I had, you were encased in ice."

Hazziq nodded, enthusiastically. "Yes, I was trapped for several days. But once the ice melted enough, I was able to free myself."

"That was quite a while ago. What have you been doing?"

"Surviving, by the grace of Dina. Day by day, all alone, until I encountered them." He nodded at the other two goblins.

Rob looked them over, and the two wilted in apprehension at his scrutiny. "Who are they?"

"They are from the Dark Leaf clan. Outcasts, like me. I found them as they crossed over the mountains. We made a camp in a cave to the east. We've been there this whole time. But, things have changed." His voice trailed off.

"Changed? How?"

"That is why we are here, to show you."

"Show me what?" Rob said, feeling slightly alarmed.

"Our village."

"Village. You have a village here? In the valley?"

"Yes, Mighty One. It is on the foot of the mountains. We have come here to ask for you to come and see it." The goblin's expression was comically expectant.

Rob sat back in the saddle, trying to digest this information. There was an entire village of goblins in his valley, and no one knew about it. Normally, such news would throw him into a panic and he would immediately set about destroying it. No one liked goblins, and they certainly weren't a race you wanted to have as neighbors.

But this was Hassiq, a peace-loving goblin he'd saved and who'd pledged a fellowship with Rob.

After several moments of thought, Rob nodded. "Okay, take me to it."

Hazziq cheered, then gathered himself together. "Sorry, friend Robert. I was worried you would not react favorably to us. Come, I will show you."

Rob hadn't reacted favorably either way, yet. He needed to see this village before deciding what to do.

After calming everyone down at the gate, and commending them for their reactions, Rob and the goblins went east; crossing the field and into the forest.

As they traveled, Hazziq asked how his kingdom was doing. Despite some hesitancy, Rob found himself giving a point by point overview of what had happened. The goblin intently listened, nodding the whole time.

Rob found the conversation strangely cathartic in some way. Up until now, he'd never spoken to anyone about his journey of building a kingdom. Everything had been internalized. Speaking about it made him feel a little less lonely.

The two spoke so intently, Rob was surprised when they suddenly walked out into a clearing to find dozens of goblins there.

Fighting back the instinct to start killing them all, Rob looked around. The goblins didn't attack, or scream in alarm at his appearance. Instead, they went about their business, moving amongst the huts which had been built there.

Racks of animal skins were set out to dry, and a female goblin was pounding a mortar and pestle, making some kind of flour.

Two tiny goblins ran around from behind a hut, laughing and playing with sticks.

Children. Goblin children.

As he took the scene in, he noticed the mouth of a large cave on the other side of the village. He recognized it as the cave he had killed the death flower in.

"Hazziq," Rob said, more than a little alarmed at what he was seeing, "there are a lot of goblins here. Where did they come from?"

"Outcasts, all of them. Each rejected by their clans, some even escaping execution, like me. All were seeking a place to escape to, away from the murder and hatred of warring clans. One by one, or in pairs, they arrived here." He gave Rob a serious look. "I was able to help them. Gradually, as our numbers grew, we built this little place. Our safe haven from the world that hates us and wants to see us destroyed. Which is why I have come to you now."

Rob felt a headache starting. "Came to me for what?"

"To ask for your official permission to stay here. To live here. We have nowhere else to go, and we've been hiding here, afraid your rangers might discover us and attack."

It was a valid concern. Had the village been discovered while Rob was in the Dead City, Jace would have had no compunction in annihilating every single goblin there.

"This is one hell of a surprise," Rob said, considering what to do. One one hand, Hazziq had proven himself a friend, even though their time together had been brief, and he felt could be trusted. On the other hand, goblins had been the scourge of the valley since the moment he arrived, until he wiped them out.

He noticed many in the village were armed, but as goblins passed him, and nodded, he didn't feel a hint of hostility. Only trepidation.

Rob sighed, running a hand over his beard. He didn't need this right now. Yet, it was something that had to be dealt with.

After a few moments of contemplation, Rob said, "Okay, Hazziq. You all can stay."

The goblin gasped, and tears formed in his large goblin eyes. "Thank you, friend Robert. I... I was very worried about what you might decide. But I'm relieved. Happy and relieved."

Rob leveled him with a serious look. "But there are conditions which need to be followed if we're going to make this work." He had no idea how he was going to explain this to Saif, let alone the people of Hope.

"Whatever they are, we will do them," Hazziq said.

Rob explained that all the goblins needed to restrict themselves to that section of the valley. It was more for their safety than limiting their movements. It would take time for the people of Anika to get used to a village of goblins in the valley. Keeping them to the northeast area would prevent any encounters with folks not yet caught up with the new dynamic.

Hazziq would be responsible for keeping some form of law and order amongst his people, and to ensure there were no problems.

Finally, Rob wanted some sort of control of the traffic over the mountains. He didn't want large groups of goblins showing up. Individuals or small families were fine. It would require Hazziq posting a lookout, or guard on the other side of the mountain, and keep it regularly manned.

All these Hazziq agreed to. But the goblin's main concern was being discovered by a roving goblin warparty. Nearly everyone in the village was marked for death, and we're terrified of being discovered. He wanted to be able to evacuate his people to Hope if the need arose.

"Of course you can," Rob said. "If trouble comes looking for you here, get everyone to town. Try and send word ahead, if you can." He looked at all the weapons being casually carried around. The village could be considered a war party on its own.

Finally, Hazziq said, "All there is left is for me to pledge fealty to you."

"Don't we already have a fellowship?" Rob didn't really know how a fellowship worked anyway.

"I want our village to be a part of the kingdom of Anika. May I?"

Rob nodded.

The Village of Safe Haven wishes to pledge fealty to you and the kingdom of Anika.

Accept? Y/N

Rob accepted, hoping it was the right thing to do.

Hazziq shook his hand. "Thank you, again, friend Robert. You will not regret this. I promise."

I better not, Rob wanted to say by way of a joke, but didn't when he saw how serious this was to the goblin. It was serious.

As Rob made his way back to Hope, he kept shaking his head in disbelief. He'd just forged an alliance with a bunch of goblins.

Explaining that to Saif was going to be fun.

CHAPTER SEVENTEEN

"We're going to need more water, my Lord. There are no two ways about it, I'm afraid," said Benson.

"How much more?" Rob asked.

"A whole lot more than we're currently getting."

Rob and the builder stood in the middle of one of the streets, watching as workers dug trenches along both sides. Others set flat bricks of stones overtop the trenches, sealing them off from above. The new sewage system was to allow wastewater to be flushed from the buildings, and into the trenches, which would then be carried out of town. But water was needed for the process to work, and there wasn't much to be had.

Rob looked over the trenches. The only water coming into town was being hand cranked from the well, just outside the southwest wall. That would need to be improved, too.

"It won't make a difference," Benson said. "We need a lot of water. Like, a torrent to manage what is being built. There are a lot of people in town now, all requiring a constant feed. The source from the well won't cut it."

Rob nodded, thinking. There was only one other source nearby. "The creek."

"That'll do it. If we can dig a channel from the creek to town, we'd have all the water we need. Fortunately, the town is more or less level with the creek so it can get here by its own power."

But digging a channel would require taking it under the wall. Benson said he could build a stone pipe access which could then be barred. The same would need to be done for the wastewater, which would be funneled further down, into the creek, and out to sea.

Rob nodded and made the adjustments in the kingdom menu. Unsurprisingly, the required resources grew, but there was no avoiding it.

"Do you have enough workers for this?" Rob said. "Digging the channel alone will take a huge effort. The creek is close, but not that close."

"With all these new arrivals streaming in, I'm up to my eyeballs in requests for jobs. Shouldn't be a problem."

Rob left the builder to his business. There had been a significant increase in people moving to Anika, especially Hope. The place was virtually bursting at the seams. Some came for a new start, but many were fleeing conflicts outside the valley, which appeared to be happening everywhere.

Everyone is fighting everyone, Rob thought. Just so long as they didn't fight him, he really wasn't concerned about events outside his kingdom. He had plenty to deal with here.

He came across Saif near the town square, talking with a man he didn't recognize.

"Ah, my Lord," Saif said. "Allow me to introduce you to Mr. Periwinkle."

Rob shook the man's hand. "Nice to meet you. Are you a new arrival in our town?"

Periwinkle said, "Oh, no, I'm not, my Lord. My residence is in Crossroads. I'm here scouting for a new location."

"A location for what?"

"Another inn."

Rob was confused. "*Another* inn. You already have one?"

"Yes, in Crossroads, next to the casino. A grand location, if I might say so."

"Casino?" Rob was flummoxed. Zuthus had built an inn and a casino in Crossroads without checking with him first?

"Yes," Periwinkle said. "Mostly cards and dice, but they're finishing up a racetrack out back which will really bring in the customers."

"To race what?"

"Pigs, as I understand it. Zuthus never said why he wanted to race pigs, but who am I to question an economic genius like him?"

Rob's mind reeled at what he was hearing. A racetrack, too? What the hell was going on down there? The troglodyte really was taking his role as leader of the village to a whole new level.

Sensing Rob's growing annoyance, Saif said, "Mr. Periwinkle was looking to start an inn, here, in Hope. Something we need."

Rob nodded. "That we do. Have you found a house to convert?"

Saif said, "Two actually, they will need to be merged. The families have already relocated outside the walls and Mr. Periwinkle has given them a generous payment."

"Great, show me," Rob said.

The two houses were a few doors down from Smiley's tavern, which was already full of patrons.

"Great location, here," Periwinkle said. "Once traveling customers get drunk enough, they're within crawling distance of the inn. It's perfect."

Saif said, "All that is needed is for you to merge the buildings, my Lord."

Rob had seen the option before, but had never used it. He selected both buildings then chose the merge option.

The two houses suddenly moved, sliding closer together until they touched. Then, he selected the convert to inn option. The entire building shuddered then went still.

"Perfect!" Periwinkle exclaimed. "I'll start renovations immediately. I hope to be open to guests within a few days. Thank you, my Lord."

The innkeeper ran off to make arrangements.

Quest completed: Inn and Out.

You have found an innkeeper to set up an inn within Hope. Now merchants and traveling dignitaries will have a place to stay.

Reward: Inn.

"The inn will make a considerable difference," Saif said as they continued down the street. "Merchants and traders will be more prone to visit, bringing economic opportunities here that might not otherwise happen."

"Sounds like it's already happening in Crossroads. Did you hear about the casino or inn before?"

"I'm afraid not. It would appear Zuthus' plans for expansion have become untethered."

Maybe they should be tethered, Rob thought. The idea of Crossroads having special buildings before Hope rubbed him the wrong way. But was he just being unreasonable? Crossroads growth was Anika's, too.

A guard appeared. "My Lord, there is a trader in the town square, demanding to see you."

"A trader? A trader in what?"

"Slaves, my Lord."

"What?" Rob said, horrified.

Saif blinked in surprise. "Slavery is a great income generator. Both in their selling and labor. Few empires have been built without them."

Rob felt his temper flare up. The very idea of slavery was abhorrent to him. "Well, my empire won't be one of them."

"But, my Lord-," Saif said.

Rob cut him off. "You surprise me, Saif. After all you went through with the Pech, how can you condone such a practice?"

He marched down the street to the town square with Saif hurrying after. In the square, he found a depressing sight.

A half-dozen humans were huddled together, chained and shackled. Chained at the end was the only non-human, a minotaur.

Standing around them, and looking bored, were four armed guards wearing expensive looking gear. A tall man, in an opulent robe, and obviously the one in charge, was berating one of the townsfolk.

"Where is the slave-block?" he said. "How can any place be considered civilized without a slave-block for auctionings? Have I stumbled into some backwater outhouse?"

Rob walked over to him. "What's going on here?"

The man turned and looked Rob over. "And who might you be?"

"I'm the king of this backwater outhouse. Who are you?"

The man's demeanor instantly changed. "Ah, well, then. Progress has been made. I am Geldhan, and I am here to offer my wares." He waved a hand at cowering slaves.

One looked up, and a guard whipped him. The man quickly looked down, again.

Rob walked over to the slaves, seething with pent up rage. Every fiber of his being wanted to kill the pompous man and his guards. It would certainly send a message.

But, as looked over the slaves, he decided on another approach.

He looked at Geldhan. "How much?"

"How much is usually determined at auction. The highest bid wins."

Rob said, "I'm not interested in any bidding. I want them all. How much?"

"No bidding?" Geldhan said, perplexed. But he then sensed an opportunity. "You wish to buy them outright? All seven?"

"That's right. How much?"

The man made a show of thinking. "Two thousand gold pieces."

"Deal," Rob said.

"My Lord!" Saif said, but flinched at Rob's look.

"Pay him," Rob said.

The square was quiet as Saif counted out the gold and handed the coin bag over. Geldhan then recounted the coins with a smirk on his face.

When finished, Geldhan nodded to Rob. "A good deal, if I may say so, your lordship. I admire someone who can come to an agreement so quickly. I will make it my personal goal to ensure you are amply supplied from this day forward."

"No, you won't," Rob said.

Geldhan looked confused. "I don't understand."

Rob said. "I am declaring slavery illegal in my kingdom." He shot the slaver with a venomous look. "From this day forward."

"What? But that's ludicrous!" Geldhan said.

Rob ignored him. "Also, no slaves will be allowed to be transported through Anika's territory."

The slaver looked shocked. "Madness! Uncivilized madness!"

"Also," Rob said, walking over to him. "Effective at sundown, today, anyone caught within the kingdom's borders practicing or dealing in slavery shall be arrested and executed."

Geldhan blanched and his guards looked around in worry.

Rob pointed a finger south. "Get the hell out of my kingdom, and don't come back."

Seeing Rob's rage, the slaver didn't try to argue. He hustled out of the square, his guards surrounding him. He got into a pretty looking wagon, pulled by oxen with silver horns, and rod off.

Rob said, "Did we get the keys from him?"

"Here," Saif said, handing them over.

Rob unlocked all seven, dropping the shackles and cuffs to the ground. They stared at him with fearful confusion.

"You're free," Rob said.

The huddled group gasped, but still looked confused, not certain what was happening was actually real.

Rob said. "You are free. You are no longer enslaved. If you wish, you can stay here in Anika. Or you can return to your homes, wherever that may be."

For several moments, the group simply stared. Then, the man who'd dared to look up, spoke. "Thank you. Thank you for saving us."

Trying to keep his emotions under control, he told Saif, "Give them each ten gold pieces, and find them fresh clothes and a meal."

"Yes, my Lord," Saif said. He wisely said nothing else.

Rob went to his manor, wanting to get out of sight. He needed a nap. He'd dealt with a lot of sewage, today. Two kinds, actually.

A message appeared.

Quest completed: Kill Quartek the Cruel.

Rob stopped, surprised. He read the rest of the message.

Quartek has succumbed to the Black Widow's poison. Although you did not directly kill the monster, you had a prominent hand in its death, and freed the swamp from its presence.

Reward: 4,500 experience points.

Rob laughed. This was totally unexpected, considering he thought he'd failed the quest.

So, today, instead of dealing with two kinds of sewage, he'd dealt with *three.*

And it felt great.

CHAPTER EIGHTEEN

Over the next week, significant progress had been made on the two main projects.

Trenton had almost finished the main floor of the Constabulary, placing finely cut stone blocks with his levitation. He was almost ready to start building up the second floor.

Kortz had already made several heavy iron bars and would have all of them ready to build cells, once Trenton gave the go ahead.

For the sewers, Benton had created a heavy work team to dig a channel from the western wall toward the creek. It was several feet wide and half a dozen deep. He said in several days, he'd begin digging the outflow channel, also, which would go under the wall to the northwest.

Everywhere Rob looked, he saw people digging, hauling and sweating with their efforts. And he saw smiles, too. Everyone was working, and they knew these projects were for their long-term benefit.

Rob couldn't help but be pleased. Yet, not for the other's reasons. What he saw was significant progress being made toward the next kingdom level. Even though the tantalizing prospect of an exploit was out there, he still needed to keep his eye on the ball.

The exploit.

He hadn't been contacted by his mysterious ally. Had his trip to the Dead City been futile? For that reason, maybe. But the Shard Garden was down there, growing Life Magic shards. Discovering the garden had certainly made it worth his while. He hoped the garden would generate enough shards so he could use the resurrection chamber whenever needed. At some point, he'll have to go back down into the city and check. If the gnolls were still there, he'd do everything to avoid them. They weren't his concern.

The lookouts placed by the sealed cave had yet to report a breach, or any sign the gnolls had traveled to the surface. Which suited Rob just fine, he just wanted to focus on Anika's progression.

And something significant happened, to that end.

One morning, Rob was busy adjusting the position of houses outside the wall, when Saif approached.

The sage had been very quiet after the incident with the slaver, and didn't bring the subject of slavery up, again.

"My Lord, a dignitary has arrived in town," Saif said. He looked positively glowing at the news.

"A dignitary?" Rob said, turning a house so it faced the morning sun better. "Like, from another kingdom?"

"No, even better than that. From a bank!"

Rob fixed the house into place, and the owner thanked him. He turned his attention to Saif. "A bank. Like a money bank?"

"Yes," Saif said, excitedly. "I believe they want to discuss establishing a branch, here, in Hope."

"Okay," Rob said. So they had banks in this universe. It made sense for there to be a place for people to safely store their money. "I guess that's good news."

"Good news!?" Saif almost squealed. "This is better than anything a young kingdom like ours could hope for."

"Why?"

"It gives Anika validity, as well as prominence on the world stage."

"Again, I have to ask, why?"

"My Lord, kingdoms which are failing don't attract the attention of banks, successful ones do. Banks will only set up in places they know for certain have the potential for growth. Or, in Anika's case, *more* growth. Having a bank will guarantee merchants and businesses will want to come here. It also significantly strengthens our ability to make secure trade deals with other kingdoms.

Outside of placing the Kingdom Cornerstone, this is the most significant step of progression which can happen."

Rob keyed into the one word he liked to hear: progression. But he still wanted to play it cool.

"Well, let's see what they have to say. Where are they?"

"I put them in the tavern."

"What? Why there?"

"Without access to the castle, there are no other appropriate places to hold such a meeting. I had Smiley clear out all the patrons beforehand."

Rob sighed. Saif was right, until he regained the castle again, there weren't many other options available.

When he and Saif arrived outside the tavern, the sage suddenly stopped him, and started adjusting Rob's garb.

"What are you doing?" Rob said, trying to swat his hands away.

"Please, you look like you've been moving buildings around all morning."

"Well, I have."

"They don't need to see that. There, that's better."

"Do I look kingly, now?"

Saif shrugged. "Kingly enough."

With a sigh, Rob entered the tavern.

Inside, he found three people sitting at one of the round tables; two men and a woman. They looked as incredibly bored as they were rich. Each had an untouched tankard of ale in front of them.

At his entrance, they turned to look at Rob. Almost immediately, their faces changed from boredom to doubt.

Before Rob could speak, Saif brushed past him.

"Gentleman, and Lady, please allow me to introduce you to the king of this fair land, his lordship, Robert Barron."

Rob opened his mouth to speak, but Saif wasn't done talking.

"Founder of the kingdom of Anika. Slayer of Quartek the Cruel. The bane of bandits. The crusher of ants..."

Rob cleared his throat.

Saif took the hint. "And the Chosen One of the gods!"

The dignitaries, who stood during the introduction, then bowed.

The woman spoke. "I am Charr, Lead Designate of the Bank of Harmony. These are my associates. It is an honor to make your acquaintance, Lord Barron."

Not certain how to properly react, he decided to wing it. Nodding to Charr, he said, "I am honored to meet you, as well, Lady Charr."

"Charr is fine, your lordship. There is no royalty in my blood. We are here in hopes of discussing business with you."

"Very good," Rob said. "Please be seated and make yourself comfortable."

He joined them at the table, noting how opulent their clothing was, even garrish. Each wore large amounts of jewelry which twinkled when they moved. These people loved their bling.

"I understand you are interested in opening a bank here in Hope?" Rob said.

Before Charr could answer, Smiley burst in from the kitchen holding two large pitchers. "Anyone in need of a top up?" he said, slopping ale.

"No, thank you," Rob said, trying not to sound annoyed.

Smiley said, "Then how about something to nibble on? Meat pies? Steamed cabbage rolls?"

"No thanks, Smiley, we're fine for now," Rob said.

Smiley said, "Finger sandwiches?"

"Not now," Rob said, through grit teeth. "Maybe later."

"I'll prepare some anyway, just in case," Smiley said, then vanished into the kitchen where pots and pans clattered about.

Rob made an effort to smile at the dignitaries. "Apologies for the interruption."

Charr said, "Our organization recognizes the growing economic potential of Anika. We would like to help you with that endeavor and open a bank branch here."

"I see," Rob said, taking a sip of his tankard. "And what help are you looking to offer?"

At his shoulder, he felt Saif tense up.

Charr said, "A myriad of opportunities, your highness. Security for your people's deposits as well as vaults for valuables."

"Vaults?"

"Yes, they will be under the bank, below ground. We've used the same bank design for centuries and find it to be the most secure.

But, as far as opportunities for the kingdom, and yourself, we would be able to offer loans, as needed. At a reasonable rate, of course."

Wow, bank people sounded all the same, regardless of the universe.

Rob nodded in thought. "So you would require a building for the branch?"

"We would construct our own. We have teams of builders specializing in our specific requirements, all with the goal of creating a very secure building. We will hire locals for general construction duties. I understand you have a Constabulary?"

Saif spoke up, "Yes, its construction is nearly completed."

"Then we would ask to be given a lot next to, or at the very least, near the Constabulary. Also, we understand kingdoms like to handle their own security matters and respect that. But any and all security within the bank building itself, will be entirely handled by us."

Rob said, "So, you'll be providing your own guards?"

"Correct. Also, both the staff and guards will need places to stay, at least until more housing becomes available."

Saif said, "That can be arranged. No issue there."

It looked to Rob like the sage was shivering with excitement.

"How soon would you be able to open the branch?" Rob said.

"Once we have your go ahead, we could have it ready within two to three weeks." She arched her brow. "Do we have your go ahead?"

They all looked at him expectantly.

To Rob, it sounded great. A bank with vaults to store his money and valuable items. Right now, he was just using the old trunk in his manor with a guard at the door.

And the access to loans had possibilities for future construction projects and even military campaigns.

It all sounded good to him. But he worried it might be a little too good. Was there an angle to the bankers presence there other than usury profits?

He glanced at Saif, who was offering a diplomatic smile of impatience. The sage nodded for him to take the deal.

If there was a downside to having a bank, he couldn't see it. And if one did come up, he'd just burn the branch down.

"You have my go ahead to open a bank," Rob said.

For the first time, everyone in the room smiled.

A message appeared.

Achievement Unlocked: Secured Deposits.

You have gotten your kingdom its first bank. A major achievement, and one which will help you and your subjects prosper.

Reward: 10,000 experience points.

Rob's smile grew bigger upon seeing how much XP he'd unexpectedly just been given.

Smiley suddenly burst into the room wielding a tray. "Care to celebrate with some scrumptious finger sandwiches?"

CHAPTER NINETEEN

"Coal, my lord," Benson said. "Black, beautiful coal."

He and Rob stood at the end of a branch in the mine, examining a newly exposed deposit of the ore.

"Fantastic," Rob said. "Any idea how much there is?"

The builder shook his head. His resemblance to his father was almost uncanny. "No way to know until we dig in deeper. I'll pull miners off the iron ore and have them focus here."

There was no worry of the kingdom running out of iron. It was positively awash in it. Kortz had so many iron ingots, he resorted to storing them in nearby houses.

And as for the blacksmiths, they would be delighted with the discovery. Real coal meant less reliance on charcoal, which apparently made smithing tougher items easier.

Paxx could finally take a break from her charcoal pit which she'd had going near continuously since their arrival.

"There is one slight problem," Benson said.

Rob chuckled. There always was. "What's that?"

"We're a short distance away from the sarcophagus. Almost level with it here. What should I do if this vein heads in that direction?"

Disturbing the sarcophagus was not an option, coal or no coal. "How far away is it?"

"In a straight line, maybe twenty paces."

Yikes. That was already too damn close for Rob's comfort. Still, they needed to see where the vein went. "Don't go more than ten paces. Maybe we'll get lucky."

"I certainly hope so, my lord."

Rob stepped outside and summoned his mount.

He was more than a little disappointed another achievement hadn't appeared with the coal's discovery. Whatever leveling goals the kingdom's hidden list had, it better have put a fat checkmark next to coal. As well as one for the bank, too.

Instead of riding straight back to town, he headed south. As he entered the swamp, a large lean-to came into view. Several guards were around it, cooking food on a fire. When they spotted Rob, they stopped what they were doing and stood at attention. To his surprise, one of them was Fenton.

"My lord," Fenton said with a little bow.

Rob dismounted. "At ease everybody. Go back to your lunch, please."

After a moment's hesitation, the guards did just that.

"What brings you here, if I may ask?" Fenton said.

"Came to check on that." He nodded at the sealed cave entrance a short distance away. It remained unchanged from when he'd last seen it.

"Nothing to report," Fenton said. "No sounds, nothing."

Rob nodded. His worry over the gnolls vacillated between disinterest or straight up paranoia. But having a guard present here helped ease his mind. And since Quartek was no longer a threat to the area, he considered increasing the guard at the cave.

"How would you feel about setting up something permanent here? Say a proper building?" Rob said.

"Do you think our presence will be needed here for a while?"

"Yes, I do." He expected the Dead City to be a factor for a long while. Not only for its Shard Garden, but also for the fact an army had river access directly beneath his kingdom. Having more security here would be prudent.

Rob selected a small single-story keep from his menu and placed it next to the camp. The outline flashed, then was gone.

"I'll get Trenton to assign workers to it right away. No need for you all to be sleeping outside anymore."

Fenton smiled. "This means you want me to increase the guard contingency as well?"

"Please. Hey, are you out here checking on things, too?"

"Actually, I just got back from checking on the last assigned watcher of the range. I'm happy to inform you all spots along the mountains, identified by the rangers as potentially risky, are now under observation. And, if we can trust the goblins to keep watch on their corner, I can confidently claim the entire valley is secure."

Quest Complete: Secure the Borders.

All potential entry points into your kingdom are now under guard and secured.

Reward: 3,000 experience points.

"Fantastic!" Rob said. "You've done a brilliant job, Fenton."

This First Ward appeared to almost blush at the praise. "Jace was a big help. Getting the watchers set up right took some doing, but we managed it."

"Any update on recruitment for the Guard?"

"More applicants than we can handle. Fortunately, it gives me a good selection to pick from. We're getting more skilled fighters into our ranks which, in turn, helps with the troops overall training."

Fenton had been running practice drills with the guard, outside the walls of town, almost daily. With the assistance of both Lessa and several experienced guardsmen. They had formations worked out, and engaged in mock combat drills. To Rob's unskilled eye, they almost looked like a functioning army. Almost.

Rob thanked Fenton and left the Ward to his business. He next went to check on the third family member of the builder clan.

The Constabulary's main building had been completed, and all that remained was its enclosing stone wall.

Rob rode up to find Trenton standing atop the wall, next to the newly placed iron gate Kortz had made.

"There you are!" Trenton bellowed, seeing him. "You have uncanny timing."

"Why is that?" Rob said, dismounting. The entire structure was daunting to look at, which helped for a police station and prison.

"I'm about to set the final stone!" Trenton held a large, rectangular stone in his meaty hands. Slowly, he squatted down and set it into place on the wall.

As it clunked into position, a message appeared.

Achievement Unlocked: Guardians of the Realm.

You have completed your kingdom's very first Constabulary, granting added security to the people of Anika.

Reward: 2,000 experience points.

Rob was delighted, twice over. Once for the building being completed, as well as for more unexpected XP.

He congratulated the builder, and the assembled workers and townsfolk cheered.

Trenton grinned. "This will also make Fenton happy, too. He'd been complaining about getting this building done for ages."

Whatever disappointment Trenton had with Fenton switching occupations seemed to be gone, which Rob was glad to see. The father and son had barely spoken to each other since Rob had made Fenton First Ward.

Trenton wiped his brow. "Guess it's time for a tankard or two."

"You've earned it," Rob said. "And after, you can get started on your next job."

"Oh, and what would that be? A huge monument to the gods? That would take years, and cost lots of gold." His eyes lit up at the prospect.

Rob laughed and told him about the keep in the swamp.

Trenton laughed. "Monuments or little keeps, I don't care which I build, just as long as I'm working."

Leaving Trenton to his ale, Rob went looking for Saif. He found him in the town square, helping to organize the townspeople to set up vegetable stalls.

Many of the locals had taken to setting up stalls outside their homes to sell whatever extra goods they've foraged or grown. Rob thought using the town square as a makeshift marketplace would work better, since it wasn't being used for anything.

"How goes it?" he asked the sage.

"Organized chaos," Said said, looking a little more flustered than usual. "Everyone thinks they know what the best spot is, and demands it for themselves, even if it's taken. Makes for an interesting day. But we'll sort it out."

Rob was about to say something, when he spotted a group of riders appear on the southern road. They ignored the gate, and went directly to the hill to ride up it. One held up Orbin's banner.

Quinn.

Rob and Saif watched as the group reappeared from behind the wall, and climbed up the hill to the castle gate. Quinn easily stood out, and his demeanor was surprising.

"Is he actually smiling?" Rob said.

"It would appear so, my Lord."

The overlord never smiled, but he looked positively joyous now. What could make such a grump grin like a fool?

"This can't be good for us," Rob said.

"Agreed. Do you think he will be punished for leaving?"

"I would expect Flint to have a stern word with him, at the very least. But whether he'll be punished, we can only hope."

Just as he was about to pass through the gate, Quinn spotted Rob. The overlord's grin widened even more, giving Rob the chills.

"No," Rob said. "Whatever he's up to, it won't be good for us at all."

CHAPTER TWENTY

"I can say the first harvest will happen in the next couple of days," Saif said. "Provided it doesn't rain, which might delay things."

"Just as long as it happens soon, I'll be happy," Rob said.

The two stood on the southern road, opposite Breddin's old farmhouse. Before them was a vast field of wheat, which extended all the way to the distant tree line. Nearby, farmers also tilled freshly exposed earth, freed up by the woodcutters.

The crop growing efforts were finally about to pay off with corn, wheat, and other grains all ready to be harvested.

"I think people are going to get a little fat after this," Rob said. He marveled at how far his kingdom had come when all there had been to eat was rats.

Saif said, "The kingdom's coffers will be fattened as well. Both Zuthus and the Crimson Council have already reserved a large share of it. But, given how much there is, I think setting up trade deals with other parties could be advised."

"Well, when I meet one of those parties, I'll be sure to mark up the price." Rob wanted to expand his business partners beyond only the troglodytes, and add another level of economic opportunity for Anika. He didn't need the animosity between Zuthus and the mountain trogs potentially affecting his income. The two ignored each other, but if that changed, he needed to be ready.

A shout made them turn toward a farmer in the field. The man pointed at the sky.

Above, to the east, two winged animals flew through the cloud cover. After a moment, Rob realized they were flying in his direction.

Dragons?! He drew his sword, and double checked his buffs. If they were dragons, all the crop fields were at risk of being burned.

Saif changed his stance, ready to cast Lightning. "My lord…"

"I see 'em." Rob felt panic rise up through his chest. What the hell were dragons doing here?

But as the creatures got closer, he saw there weren't dragons at all. They were feathered with the heads of eagles, and had four clawed legs.

Griffins.

Not certain if they were a threat, he blinked in surprise when he noticed each had a rider on their back.

Human looking, with dark skin and long, pointed ears. They reminded him of Myna, the elf woman who'd taught him his sweep ability so long ago.

Only these were taller in frame, and had skin as black as coal.

Just as the griffins descended to within range of Rob's Sun-Bolt, one of the elves called out.

"Hello, there! We're friendly! We mean you no harm!"

Rob and Saif glanced at each other, uncertain.

The elf said, "We would like to speak with you! Is it okay if we land?"

Rob shrugged. At least they weren't attacking. "Okay!" He sheathed his sword, but kept a hand on the pommel.

With tremendous, flapping wings, the large beasts landed on the road. Other than having four legs, and an elongated body, they were exactly like a bald eagle.

The two elves dismounted. Each wore exquisite armor, and had huge swords strapped to their backs. The weapons glowed from within their sheaths.

As the tall beings approached, Rob tried to look them over.

Dark elves.

When he attempted to ascertain their level, he practically went cross eyed. It was like trying to look into the sun.

Rob swallowed. These two were so high a level, either one could lay waste to the entire valley, and everything in it, without breaking a sweat.

"Apologies if we startled you," one of them said. "You're Robert Barron, correct?"

"I am," Rob said.

Saif spoke up. "King of Anika. Slayer of Quartek the Cruel. Squasher of ants..."

Rob glared at the sage.

"And Chosen One of the gods," Saif quickly finished.

"Wow," the elf said. "Quite impressive."

"Who are you?" Rob said. He couldn't take his eyes off the griffins. Flying mounts. Where could he get one of those?

"I'm Trin, this is my brother, Drin."

"Pleased to make your acquaintance," Drin said with a slight bow.

Both elves giggled.

Rob sensed a certain level of mockery, but ignored it. "What brings you to Anika?" Hopefully not conquest. If so, Rob would surrender, right then and there. Compared to him, they appeared practically godlike.

Trin said, "My brother and I are adventurers. When we're not plowing through dungeons, we like to take a break and jump into the nearest Annex anomaly. We notice you have one here."

"The Annex Marsh?" Rob said.

"Is that what you call it? Different locations have different names. We would like to use yours, if we may."

"Use it?" Rob said, a little aghast. "You want to go *into* the Annex Marsh? Like, intentionally?"

The brothers giggled, again; a strange, high pitched sound.

Trin said, "Yes, of course. The anomalies are always a bit of fun."

Bit of fun? The Annex Marsh? Rob's mind reeled. "Usually I avoid the place. It's a deathtrap. Why would you want to go in there?"

"Loot," said Trin.

"Fun," said Drin.

Rob tried not to laugh at the idea. Yet, these two were of such a high level, maybe the place wasn't that big a threat to them. "You're obviously aware of how dangerous it is."

"Of course," Trin said. "There is always a risk of something going wrong, I suppose."

Drin said, "Which is why we specifically came to use your entry point."

"Why's that?"

Drin said, "We understand that, as the Chosen One, you have access to the ability of resurrection at the altars. Is that true?"

Rob didn't expect that as a topic of conversation. "Yes. With some limits."

"But you can do it, right?"

"Yes, but I've only done it once before. Why do you ask?"

The brothers exchanged a look.

"I told you it was true!" Trin said.

"Did I say I doubted you?" Drin said. "I don't believe I did."

Trin looked at Rob. "So, if we die, you can bring us back, correct?"

"Technically, yes. As long as the person is known to me, and their name appears on the list of candidates to resurrect."

Drin said, "Well, you know our names now."

Trin said, "We've become acquainted. That should suffice, don't you think?"

"I'd need five Major Shards of Life magic, too. Each. If you manage to get out alive, I get to keep them."

"Fair enough," Drin said, rummaging through the most glamorous hip pouch Rob could imagine. "Here you go."

Rob took the ten shards. Then said, "Also, twenty five thousand gold apiece, non-refundable. Whether you die or not."

The elves didn't so much as blink at the amount as Trin pulled out a huge coin bag.

"Does that include the entry fee?" Trin said, while counting.

"Five thousand, each, for the entry fee," Rob said, trying not to grin.

The elf handed a coin bag with sixty thousand gold, in total. He should have asked for more!

Rob said, "Just one thing, though. If you die, I can only resurrect you once every day."

"I hope we don't die very often," Drin said, and they giggled.

Rob said, "And I do it when I'm here, in the valley. If I have to go away, you'll need to wait for my return."

Both elves nodded in unison.

"Sounds like a small price to pay for another chance at life," Trin said.

The two elves gracefully mounted their griffins.

"Oh, we wanted to pick up some food. Where's the nearest market?" Drin said.

Rob pointed north. "In Hope, at the town square. But, I'd ask for you to walk your mounts through the front gate. Flying in might terrify everyone."

The elves giggled, then launched into the air. Rob and Saif watched in wonder as they flew north.

"That was cool," Rob said.

"And profitable," Saif said, shaking the coin bag. "You just made sixty thousand in gold for doing nothing."

"I wonder how many adventurers like those two who are willing to pay for a resurrection?"

Saif smiled. "I believe we just created another source of revenue for the kingdom, my lord."

If rich, suicidal lunatics wanted to give Rob shards and bags of coins for the service, he'd be happy to do it.

Rob said, "If they do get out of the Annex alive, they'll probably have loot and treasure on them. Maybe they'd be willing to sell or trade what they don't want." He thought of all the item possibilities within the high level Annex, and started to drool.

Yet, again, there wasn't a message of achievement for coming up with this new revenue source. He hoped another big, fat checkmark was being put in his kingdom leveling list.

He felt a level up was in order, but none came.

What else was he expected to do?

CHAPTER TWENTY ONE

"I had five slaves. Do you realize how much having them would have saved me over time? More than I care to think about!" Zuthus said.

"I don't care. There'll be no slavery in Anika at all. Period," Rob said.

He and Zuthus were standing in one of the troglodyte's newer warehouses. Its shelves were steadily filling up with goods, even as Rob watched as workers constantly carried goods in.

"No slaves just means more work for everyone else to do," Zuthus said. "I'm almost overwhelmed now with orders, and lack the people to handle it."

Rob held no sympathy for the trader. He'd ensured the trog had been compensated the full purchase price for the freed slaves. But, apparently, he needed to whine about it for a while, much to Rob's chagrin.

"Why do you have so much stuff, anyway?" Rob said, looking around. "How can the kingdom be in such need of all this?"

"You're not my only customer," Zuthus said, checking a bin of apples against a list on a long scroll he had. "There are other people and places who want these goods.

"As you know, goods pass through the kingdom en route to other destinations. Some I buy outright, then sell elsewhere."

Rob was very much aware of the cross-trade his kingdom offered. Supply trains and merchants used Anika's west and south passes to get to their destinations.

So, he recently started to tax anything passing through for the privilege. One gold piece for a wagon or cart. Ten silver pieces for any horse, mule, or other creature carrying a burden. And one silver piece for anyone, or anything, traveling by foot.

And it turned out, Anika was so strategically located, road tax revenue started to steadily stream in. Even the eastern pass, which was seldom used, still generated some taxes.

So Zuthus selling his goods to anyone other than Anika didn't irk Rob that much. The kingdom would always get its tax.

But what annoyed Rob was the horrific markup the trog tried to get away with. Some items spiked in price by two or three hundred percent. And it had to take a visit by 'the king' to get the price back down.

Rob said, "Do you charge sky-high prices to your other customers, too?"

"Only the ones I can get away with doing so."

"But the price of your beef has almost tripled. People are complaining."

Zuthus sighed. "If I discount beef, will you let me get back to work?"

"Yes. Fifty percent."

"Thirty."

"Forty."

"Done. Now if you will excuse me," Zuthus said, and quickly left the warehouse.

Rob felt like he'd achieved a minor victory. Usually it took more yelling to get his way.

Outside, he found wagons trundling by, some with supplies for distant lands, others for Zuthus's warehouses.

Lessa wandered over to him, eating what looked like a candy apple on a stick.

"Where did you get that?" Rob said.

"One of the little food stalls," she said while munching. "Cheap and good, just how I like things."

Some of the more enterprising folk in Crossroads had set up little stalls outside their homes to offer food items to the passing wagons. Ale, cooked meat, thrushberry pies, and candy apples.

Lessa finished and tossed the stick. "So was yelling at Zuthus the only thing on the agenda today? I could go back to whipping my archers if you want."

"I want to take a quick trip over the eastern pass."

"What for?" she said, frowning. "I hear it's a nightmare."

"To survey it, first-hand. But I also want to see if I can find Peter on the other side. He may have information on what Quinn was up to over there."

The temporary disappearance of the overlord greatly worried him. Rob wanted to know what he had gotten up to in the eastern region.

And it also didn't look like Quinn had been disciplined, either. At least, looking at the situation from the outside. He hadn't been flogged, or made to do laps around the town walls naked, making it hard to tell.

So a trip east was warranted.

Just then, he spotted a minotaur riding a huge horse leading a line of wagons from the south. It was Hayman. Seeing Rob, he rode over.

"You have a problem," the trader said by way of greeting.

"I do?" Rob said. "What is it?"

Looking annoyed, the minotaur dismounted, his hooves clumping loudly on the hard ground.

"Some opportunist has set up a toll on the other side of the pass," he said, hitching a thumb south.

"What? Who?"

Hayman shrugged. "Dunno. They look like a small contingent who broke off from a horselord clan, but they're just another form of bandits to me. They're charging a fee on everyone coming or going."

Rob sighed. First, it was roadside bandits, now, it was bandits in the pass.

Hayman said, "But, like I said, you have a problem. Whatever I end up paying, I just have to add to my final totals."

Rob felt a headache start. "How many are there? Are they well armed?"

"About thirty at the pass entrance, but there were at least a couple dozen riding around on horseback. Anyway, I have to see Zuthus. Good luck."

Rob thanked him as he led his wagons away.

Lessa said, "They must have just set up today, or we would have heard about it."

"Yup," Rob said. Looked like his trip east had to be delayed. This problem had to be dealt with immediately before it had a negative effect on the kingdom's economy.

Rob summoned Henry. "Let's go have a chat with our new neighbor."

CHAPTER TWENTY TWO

They rode south, out of Crossroads. Before reaching the border checkpoint, Rob took a quick detour to Perch.

There, he bound himself to the resurrection altar in the cave. If something went wrong, he didn't want to have to ride all the way down from Hope, again.

With that done, they went to the checkpoint.

About a dozen guards manned its tower and fence gateway. They took people's names and charged the road tax.

The commander there was relieved to see him. "Everyone coming through is upset," she said. "First they pay a fee to enter the pass, then a road tax when they reach us. I sent word when we found out about them."

Rob looked at the annoyed expressions of the wagon drivers, who just arrived. "Have they been there all day?"

"No, people only started to complain about it a little over an hour or two ago."

Rob said, "Okay, keep things flowing, we're going to check it out."

He and Lessa continued south. High mountains towered on either side, giving the claustrophobic sensation of closing in.

It was the first time he'd been in any of the passes, something he should have done for each, ages ago.

They passed several people heading north on foot. All took a moment to complain about the new fee, before continuing on.

At roughly the halfway point of the pass, an old landslide blocked half of the road. There was still room for carts and wagons to move around it without issue, but Rob noted the partial obstruction as something that should be removed.

Finally reaching the end of the pass, they stopped when the entrance came into view.

Ahead, a makeshift fence of logs had been erected across the road. Around it stood a large group of guards. Each were armed, and wore various kinds of leather armor.

Past them, in the distance, was a vast, rolling plain.

When the guards spotted them, they all turned to look. For several minutes, the two parties stared at each other.

"They know who you are," Lessa said.

"They had to know I'd show up," Rob said, double checking his buffs.

Lessa smiled. "I think things are about to get exciting."

They spurred their mounts forward at a casual pace, wary of an ambush.

Getting closer revealed the guards were scruffy looking, covered in dirt and had wild, unkempt hair.

Reaching the gate, Rob and Lessa stopped. The plains opened up on both sides of the pass, with distant mountains to the west, probably the same range continuing down from Anika valley.

To the southeast, away from the road, appeared to be a settlement of some kind.

All this, he took in with a few quick glances, but his main focus was on the guards.

There were easily two dozen present, some at the fence, while the rest were around campfires used for cooking.

But what really grabbed his attention were the cluster of horses grazing next to the camp. There was one horse for every person there.

They really were a horse clan.

One of the guards, a tall grizzly looking fellow, walked in front of them. "There is a toll to be paid. One gold piece each."

One gold. That really was highway robbery.

Rob ignored him, and shouted so everyone could hear. "I want to speak to whoever is in charge!"

The grizzly man snorted. "I'm in charge. Your royal highness can speak to me."

"What's your name?"

"Glemp, of the Dust Rider Clan. And you're Robert, king of whatever you got going on north of here."

The guards laughed.

Rob said, "You're blocking my pass and extorting the people trying to use it."

Glemp laughed. "Might be your pass, but this dirt we're standing on is our land. Our land, our gate. Our gate, our business."

The dirty man had a point, Rob had to give him that. He tried another approach.

"You're charging an insane fee. Why don't you reduce it to something more reasonable?" Rob could tolerate a smaller fee, if it meant keeping the peace. Looking the horse clan members over showed them to be close, if not equal, in strength to the gnolls.

Another guard laughed, and said, "Glemp, is this royal tart calling you unreasonable? How about this, then. Why don't you give us some of that gold you got hidden away up your bunghole?"

The guards laughed, and all the other horse clan members gathered around to see what would happen.

Rob and Lessa tensed, ready for a fight.

Suddenly, one of the clansmen shouted. "She's coming!"

Instantly, the group backed off. Rob knew the tension hadn't been reduced, just delayed.

To the southeast, from the direction of the settlement, came a large group of riders on horses. Plumes of dust kicked up in their wake.

As they got closer, Rob saw the leader was a woman on a magnificent, rust colored horse.

She rode up to the gate, the other riders swarming about as if they couldn't stop.

Her arrival tripled the number of clansmen, far more than could be handled.

"Do we have someone unwilling to pay?" she bellowed, glaring at Rob.

She was as dirty as the others, and brandished a long, metal spear of some kind. What little leather armor she wore exposed more than it protected.

"This royal fool," said Glemp.

Rob said, "I'm Robert. King of Anika. Who are you?"

"I'm Shanna, and we horsefolk don't care what you call yourself. We have no king, or queens. We just rule by strength. And our strength says you must pay!"

That brought a hardy cheer from the assembled throng, who were now itching for a fight.

"I'm not here to pay anything. I'm asking for you to reduce the fee," Rob said. He knew whatever he said would be futile, but felt he had to at least try.

"Ha!" Shanna shouted. "Do you hear what the king asks? Does that sound like a man of strength?"

"No!!" The horsemen roared, and waved their weapons in the air.

Okay, time to go, Rob thought. With a glance at Lessa, they backed up their mounts, and turned to leave. Both were ready to spin about if pursued.

"Ha! Look! Look at the king run away!" Shanna yelled. "Go get your gold! We want all of it!"

The two made as dignified a retreat as could be managed with a horde of wildmen screaming at them. But, they weren't pursued.

Shanna continued her verbal tirade, mostly incomprehensible above the shouting. But Rob did catch her saying one thing.

"Next time you come before the Dust Rider Clan, bring an army!"

Good idea.

CHAPTER TWENTY THREE

"I have to say, they do look impressive," Fenton said.

"That they do. Now to see how they are in battle," Rob said.

The two stood in the fields on the eastern side of Hope. Assembled before them were all the town's guards and rangers, brought together to form Anika's first true army.

Rob had further broken them up into three units, based on weapon type; archers, spears, then melee weapons.

In total, there were one hundred and fifty soldiers, not including another thirty waiting in Crossroads. As a result, Hope would have to be guarded by a skeleton crew.

Rob found it hard to think of them as soldiers. He'd gotten to know them as his subjects, and recognized many of their faces. Seeing any of them die would be difficult.

There was the uncertainty of the resurrection list. If they died, and he knew them, could they be brought back? Something told him no, only those deemed important by the game could be. But he didn't want to dwell on that. He just hoped, after this, he wouldn't need a lot of Life shards.

Saif appeared, looking somber. "Everything is ready, my lord. The nearby populace is within the town walls and the gates will be closed when you leave. Are you certain I shouldn't come?"

Erring on the side of caution, Rob wanted everyone to remain in the town while they were away. He knew the game might try something, and wanted to minimize the risk of something going wrong.

"I need you here," he said. "With Fenton leading the troops, you and Jace must protect Hope, in case of a surprise."

Saif nodded.

Rob knew the sage was secretly cheering with glee. Using an army was the first step in the grand plan to have Rob conquer the world, or whatever.

But he didn't care about any grand plan. He had his own, and that involved the exploit. Until something definitive came from that, he would go through the motions of being a good king.

With everything ready, Rob nodded and Fenton bellowed an order to march.

The assembled column, four abreast, marched through the field and onto the road, heading south. Fenton marched in front, and to the side, keeping an eye on everyone. Rob and Lessa were a little further ahead on their mounts.

At the rear of the column followed four ox driven wagons, filled with tents and supplies.

Roughly an hour before sundown, they passed through Crossroads, picking up the other town's guard. Villagers gaped at them in surprise and amazement. Even Zuthus came out of his office to stare.

When they reached the border checkpoint, Fenton gave the order to stop, then dismissed them to make camp.

Rob watched as everyone went about their assigned duties. In short order, a bustling camp was made with tents and cook fires.

He found it hard to sleep that night. Was this the right action to take? Should he have tried harder at diplomacy? Doubts swirled through his mind, but an answer never came.

The army was woken two hours before dawn. Told to leave the camp as it was, they assembled into the column, using Light spells to see.

When finally ready, they marched into the pass. No one spoke above a whisper, and efforts were made to minimize the noise of their gear.

As they passed the midway point with the landslide, Rob whispered to Fenton.

"This will be our fallback position. We can use the landslide to guard any retreat." He hoped it wouldn't be necessary, but he needed to be prudent.

"Shall I post some archers here, now?" Fenton asked.

"No. We need everyone with us."

The column continued, until it reached a slight turn in the pass. The section ahead was a straight path to the entrance, and in view of the guards.

Rob stopped and raised a hand. The column halted, canceling all Light spells, and sinking the pass into the dull gloom of the morning. The sun had only just started to rise.

Lessa dismounted and went to peek around the turn. After several moments, she returned.

"I don't see any guards, at all. The fence and camp is still there, but no one is watching the entrance."

And why would they? The Anika checkpoint only opened at dawn, and closed just after sundown. No traffic was allowed at night.

The clansmen wouldn't be expecting any traffic until first light, and probably wouldn't bother posting a guard.

Lessa said, "The coast is clear. Let's hit 'em."

She and Fenton looked expectantly at Rob.

This was the big moment, and any doubts he had the night before had to be put aside. It was do or die time.

"Okay," he said, nodding to Fenton. "You know what to do."

"Yes, my lord," Fenton said with a wry grin, and motioned to the column.

Summoning his shale-mites, Rob and Lessa rode around the turn and headed directly at the gate. Behind, the column went into a light jog. No one spoke. They'd been briefed on what to do before leaving camp.

As Rob drew closer to the gate, he watched anxiously for any signs of movement from the camp.

When he and Lessa got to within a hundred paces away, they kicked their mounts into a full run. Behind them, the column did the same.

It was a mad dash to reach the camp before being discovered. Something that couldn't be done during the daytime.

As Rob came within a dozen paces of the log fence, a groggy clansman poked his head out of the closest tent.

The man rubbed his eyes and blearily looked around. He saw Rob and Lessa vault over the fence and into the camp, and his eyes bugged out.

"An attack!" the man screamed. "We're being attacked!" Then he took an arrow to the throat.

Clansmen suddenly leapt up from bedrolls, or emerged from tents, looking around in confusion.

And Rob and Lessa were among them, shooting and hacking from their mounts. The two pushed through to the opposite side of the camp, keeping all eyes on them, and away from the pass entrance.

It worked a little too well. What grogginess and confusion the clansmen had was quickly gone, and they attacked.

For several moments, Rob could only focus on his opponents. They were skilled, countering and dodging some of his swings. But, as he fought, he heard a roaring noise which grew louder.

The column reached the entrance at a full run, and swarmed through the gate. Melee fighters led the attack, while the arches hung back by the fence, firing constantly.

The fight was on, and for several moments it was pure chaos.

Hearing a distant cry, Rob blasted a clansman in the face with Sun-Bolt, then wheeled Henry around to look.

From the distant settlement, a horde of riders came. Shanna led their charge, screaming bloody murder.

Good.

Cleaving the head of an attacker, Rob rose in his seat and shouted as loud as he could.

"Form up! Form up!"

Lessa took up the call, as well.

Quickly, Anika's force pulled out of the camp, fighting all the way, and formed up in front of the entrance.

The sneak attack had been so effective, nearly all the clansmen had been killed, many before they could arm themselves.

"Form up!" Rob continued to shout as his troops took up their preassigned positions within the mouth of the pass.

The archers stayed back, with the spearman lining the fence. All other melee warriors stood in front. The entire group formed a defensive semicircle.

And just in time.

Shanna and her screaming horde reached the camp and charged forward. The anger in their voices was palpable, but Shanna's screams drowned all of them out. Her eyes were wide with pure rage.

Lessa vaulted over the fence to join the archers. Rob dismissed Henry, and quickly stood at the very middle of the melee fighters.

Shanna and her riders quickly passed through the camp, all while taking arrow fire.

As she led them at full charge into battle, Rob suddenly shouted, "Now! Now! Now!"

He, and all the melee fighters quickly backed up to the fence, and the spearmen lunged forward between them.

Spears and riders slammed into each other with shouts and screams, and the fighters immediately engaged.

For his part, Rob swung his sword as fast as he could manage. With everyone at such close quarters, it was hard to miss. But the clansmen had high hit points, and took many successful hits to kill.

For several minutes, the two armies fought, entangled with each other along the fence.

As Rob finally hacked a clansman to his death, Shanna loomed before him, her steed rearing. She aimed her spear at his head.

Rob launched forward with a shout, and Shield-Bashed the animal in the chest.

The horse tumbled over, tossing Shanna. But she nimbly landed on her feet, and attacked Rob.

It took everything he had to keep from being skewered, parrying with his sword, or blocking with the shield. The two combatants still managed to hit each other, and blood flowed from wounds across their bodies.

Then Rob saw an opportunity. As Shanna was pulling back from a lunge, he managed to cast Sun-Bolt directly into her face.

She peeled away, screaming in agony. But he'd only struck her on the jaw and neck, missing the eyes.

But it hurt enough to force her to suddenly backpedal, whistling loudly.

Her steed raced into the throng, and she quickly leapt onto its back. She let out a high pitched trilling cry, and raced off.

Immediately, her surviving riders pulled away from the fighting to run after her.

His fighters, filled with bloodlust, shouted and chased after them.

"No! Go back!" Rob shouted. He summoned Henry and rode out to block them. "Form up again! Go! Form up!"

Charging out was what Shanna wanted. With their maneuverability, her riders could easily surround and cut his troops down.

Mercifully, his troops listened and quickly retreated back. The fence area was choked with dead and wounded. Men and horses lay tangled together, blood everywhere.

At first glance, Rob couldn't tell how many were his or the enemy, but most of the dead appeared to be clansmen.

Shanna shouted, and Rob turned to look.

Having recovered, she sat at the front of her riders, and glared at Rob, a short distance away. Then, she raised her spear. They were going to charge again.

"Get ready!" Rob shouted, dismissing Henry.

But the clansmen didn't charge at them.

Instead, Shanna made a slow sweeping motion with her spear, and the dust around her kicked up.

Uh oh.

Suddenly, a thick dust cloud appeared and raced toward the pass entrance. From the dust cloud emerged dozens of huge horses, each easily three times the size of a normal horse and ethereal in form. And all galloping at full speed directly at the entrance and his little army.

"Look out!" Rob shouted, and tried to run out of the way.

He jumped at the last second, just as the ghostly stampede crashed headlong into him.

The next moment, he was under the horses. Dust obscured his vision as huge hooves stomped around him. He caught one in the face, and his head snapped back.

Then the nightmare stampede was gone, blinking out of existence.

Rob blinked through the pain in his head, to see Shanna racing forward with her riders.

Quickly, Rob took out an item he had at the ready and pointed at the ground close to the fence.

You have used the Mobile Ant Mound.

Instantly, a mound of dirt surged up from the ground, and mutant ants swarmed out from its entrance.

Shanna shrieked as she tried to yank her horse into another direction, but she ended up slamming into the mound.

Dozens and dozens of angry, dog-sized ants attacked, covering her and her horse.

Other riders tried to wheel away, but they'd been so clustered together for the charge, most couldn't. Ants attacked them, bringing many crashing to the ground.

This happened directly in front of the fence, and Rob's stunned soldiers.

Rob wiped blood from his eyes and raised his arm. "Attack! Attack!"

The army of Anika fell upon the enemy riders.

For several minutes, ants and armies fought, but the outcome was inevitable.

Rob used sweep to knock back two clansmen, then killed them both with a follow up swing. As he finished, he saw Shanna run by, covered in ants and shrieking.

He lunged forward with his sword, and skewered her through the heart. She collapsed, dead.

Instantly, the ants on her body scampered off in search of other prey.

Her death took the fight out of the remaining clansmen. Desperate to escape, those that could rode off, while those without a mount were killed.

Rob looked at the carnage around him. Bodies and dust were everywhere. But there were no more clansmen to fight.

He spotted both Fenton and Lessa, and was relieved to see them alive. But many weren't so lucky.

The battle was over.

CHAPTER TWENTY FOUR

The wounded were attended to, and there were many. Some were able to simply cast heal on themselves, while others needed health potions.

Rob handed out all of his and cast heal while drinking mana potions.

Some of the wounds were horrific. He was used to seeing his own and was unphased. But his soldiers had never encountered such bloodshed before, and had difficulties just healing them without getting sick.

While this went on, Rob posted a picket group of healthy soldiers to keep watch for a potential ambush. What few riders who remained might come back with friends.

Rob found Fenton helping a spearman who'd nearly been cut in half at the waist. He held a potion for him to drink. As the spearman guzzled it down, his wounds slowly knitted themselves together. If there was one good thing about this universe, it was wounds that didn't kill you outright could be healed.

"How are you?" Rob asked Fenton. The young man was covered in blood, but none was his own.

"Not a scratch on me," Fenton said. He looked down at the spearman's severed belly. "It's the strangest thing. I fought and killed, but I wasn't hit even once."

The young man had a faraway look in his eyes. Rob knew he had been wounded today, but not physically. "You did great. We won because of all the training you put them through. Without that, we would have lost."

He didn't exaggerate. The discipline instilled into the soldiers had made all the difference. If everyone had run around wildly, the army would have been wiped out.

Fenton stood and looked at the dead bodies all around. "Not good enough. They didn't make it."

Rob wanted to say it was the cost of war, but knew how callus it would sound. He put a hand on Fenton's shoulder. "There are a lot of people alive because of you. Come, let's heal the rest."

It took two hours to get all the wounded fixed up. While that happened, Rob arranged to separate his dead from the enemies. The Anika dead were lined up in rows next to the road, while the clansmen were ignored.

Rob counted the bodies. Twenty eight.

That was twenty eight people he may or may not be able to resurrect. He wouldn't know for certain until he checked, but he suspected most, if not all, wouldn't be on the list.

As he looked over their still faces, he tried to tell himself this was all just a game, and none of them were real. But he still felt a well of guilt rush up inside him.

It's just a game, damnit. Keep it together!

Lessa came over to him. She, too, was smeared in blood. "So, we wait?"

"Wait for what?" Rob said.

"For their bodies to be claimed by the gods. Some folk put them in a shallow grave until then, as a way to give the dead dignity, but there's too many, and we're exposed out here."

Rob had to remind himself only those who die of old age need to be buried. Everyone else's bodies eventually despawned.

"We'll wait, then."

Fenton went to each body and said a silent prayer over each one. Others did the same.

Rob went to Shanna's corpse, which was covered in the most horrific bite marks imaginable. She lay slumped over on the ground. Even in death, her face was contorted in rage.

"How was that for a show of strength?" he asked her.

He found her metal spear nearby and picked it up.

Spear of the Steed.

Damage: 10 - 15 hit points.

+5 to Ghost Stampede.

Adds 5 more steeds to the Ghost Stampede spell.

Value: 1,000 gold pieces.

Ghost Stampede spell? So that's what she hit them with. Most of the deaths were caused by those ghostly horses stomping on the already injured. He very much wanted to know where he could learn that spell.

He pulled a necklace with a medallion off her neck.

Medallion of Mana.

+20 mana points to maximum mana.

Value: 250 gold pieces.

Nice! This was what he needed, and slipped it on.

She also had a fat coin bag with eight thousand gold pieces.

Out of respect for the dead, they patiently waited for the bodies to despawn. Doing anything else didn't feel right to Rob, and he got the sense the others felt the same way.

He reviewed the messages he'd gotten after the chaos.

Achievement Unlocked! Blood On The Battlefield.

You have won your first, true battle using an army. Learn from it as there are many more battles to come.

Reward: 5,000 experience points.

This was immediately followed by him hitting his next character level of nine.

This time around, he focused on his mana. He kept running out during fights and desperately needed more. He put all three attribute points into Intelligence, and all five skill points into Magical Affinity, increasing his mana pool.

After two hours, the bodies began to vanish, one by one, in the order they'd died. Each left behind all their clothes, armor and weapons.

The same happened to the clansmen, and their horses.

Soon, they stood within a large field of gear and clothing.

Fenton had everyone gather everything up into neat piles, sorted by item.

Once that was done, Rob told Fenton to send a messenger back to Crossroads and tell them what had happened, and to send wagons to pick up the gear. He also wanted him to arrange a large, permanent guard on this entrance. All border check duties would be handled on this end of the pass from now on.

When Rob was done, Lessa asked, "What now? Pursue the survivors?"

"Not worth it. There had been only six or seven of them that ran off."

She nodded. "Yeah. Nothing to worry about. Unless they have friends."

Rob pointed at the distant settlement. "Let's go see what their deal is."

Leaving the army behind, he and Lessa mounted up and rode toward the settlement. Rob wasn't worried about an ambush. The flatness of the plains made it impossible to surprise anyone without being spotted a couple miles out. If another horde of clansmen appeared, they'd see them.

On the outskirts, they looked over the settlement from a small rise.

It comprised about thirty small huts, and other single story buildings. Three dusty roads met at a point in the middle, where a stone well was located.

As uninteresting a place if there ever was, it had one prominent feature.

On the eastern side of the village was a large corral which looked to hold dozens and dozens of horses.

More than a little intrigued, Rob led them to the central well. They passed huts where villagers peeked out at them from hiding places.

When they reached the well, a woman came out of a nearby building which was larger than all the rest.

"Is she gone? Did you drive her away?"

Rob said, "If you mean Shanna, she's dead. We killed her."

"And the rest of her clan," Lessa added.

The woman suddenly burst into laughter. "Oh, thank the gods, she's dead! Thank you! Thank you!"

Hearing the news, other villagers timidly emerged from hiding and crowded about. They didn't look like Dust Rider Clansmen. They were very clean, and had their hair pulled up in elaborate braids.

Rob dismounted and the woman rushed over to kiss his hand.

Surprised, and a little put off by the gesture, he gently pulled his hand away.

She said, "My name is Yannal, and our village had been put under the servitude of those Dust Rider savages. They showed up a few days ago and took over the place. They kicked people out of their homes, and stole our horses. What a bunch of unwashed, horse-suckers!"

Many of the villagers nodded their heads and mumbled in agreement.

Yannal continued. "After they stole everything of value, they realized we didn't have much, so they decided to blockade the pass and extort money from travelers. They thought they'd get rich, but all they got was dead!"

Yannal danced about and the villagers cheered.

"My name is Robert," Rob said. "This is my head archer, Lessa."

Yannal stopped dancing. "We know who you are, King Robert of Anika. You are the Slayer of Quartek the Cruel, Squasher of ants..."

"And the Chosen One of the gods," the villagers shouted, almost in unison.

Rob laughed. "You can just call me Robert, if you like."

"We would like to call you more than that, King Robert. Here, let me show what we can offer."

She led them down one of the dusty streets to the huge stockade. Horses ran around inside, where men, no older than boys, rode some.

Yannal said, "We, of the Horse Head clan, have trained horses for generations. We catch wild horses on the plains, break them, then train them. See, over there?"

She pointed at a distant dust cloud, beneath which horses galloped together. There had to be over a hundred of them.

Yannal grinned at Rob. "We can offer you horses, as many as you need. All I ask is for your protection from any more roving, horse-sucking clans."

Rob looked at all the horses in the stockade. This was exactly what his kingdom needed. And his army, too. With horses, he could have cavalry. It was a no brainer.

"Yes, I will protect you."

Yannal cheered, again, then said, "And, we here in Horse Head village, give you our undying fealty."

A message appeared.

Achievement Unlocked! Expansion Is The Key.

Congratulations, you have successfully expanded your kingdom beyond its original borders. More expansion will be needed. There is an entire world out there, waiting to be conquered.

Reward: 5,000 experience points.

Almost immediately, Rob felt a tingling sensation throughout his body. It pulled at him, like invisible strings, in one direction. North.

His kingdom was ready to level up. The requirement list had finally been triggered by accepting the village into his kingdom.

Curious, he took out his map book. It showed that the border of Anika now extended past the mountains and southward. In fact, it appeared everything as far as his eye could see was now his. It may have been a lot of flat plains, but it was his now.

He had mixed feelings about it, though. Sure, he'd met one of the leveling requirements, but now he needed to keep it. That was a lot of empty land he had to suddenly protect.

But that was something he would figure out later. For now, he only wanted one thing.

He wanted to go home.

CHAPTER TWENTY FIVE

His army marched through Crossroads to cheers from the villagers. Yannal had given Rob fifty trained horses, so many of the troops were now mounted, but not as many as he liked. Riding was a skill which had to be learned, and if he was to have cavalry, more soldiers would need to be trained.

The traffic which had been halted because of the fighting, was finally able to continue through the pass.

They marched out of Crossroads, and up the central road.

Rob wondered if this was what it felt like to be one of those Roman generals returning to Rome after a successful campaign in Gaul. His army may not be as large as a Roman one, but it still felt good to be at the head of it.

As they got closer to Hope, they passed some foragers by a nearby treeline. The foragers stopped to wave and cheer.

Rob waved back. Even though he didn't even want to be in this world, he tried to enjoy the moment.

Suddenly, one of the foragers broke from the group and rushed toward the column.

Rob recognized her as Greta.

"No time!" Greta shouted, but in a man's deep voice. "There's no time!"

Quickly, Rob rode to her.

The woman suddenly tripped on her apron full of berries and tumbled to the ground.

Rob leaped from Henry, and reached out to help her up.

Greta grabbed his wrist with surprising strength, and looked at him with another person's eyes.

It was his ally!

"I have no time," Greta said. "Listen, the exploit is linked to the Great Circle somehow. You must complete it!"

"Complete it?" Rob repeated. "What do you mean?"

But Greta had looked away, as if seeing something. "Damn, they found me!"

She suddenly collapsed, shutting her eyes.

Rob shook her shoulders. "Complete it how?"

After a few moments, her eyes opened and she was Greta, again.

She looked around confused. "Oh, my Lord. How did I get here? What happened?"

"You just fell," Rob said, helping her up.

Some of the other foragers guided her back to the treeline.

Rob returned to the column, aware that everyone had seen what had happened, and was watching him in confusion.

"What, by the Many-Hells, was that about?" Lessa said as they resumed moving.

"Just an update," he said, but didn't explain. It was what he had been eagerly waiting on: confirmation the exploit was real.

If he felt good before, he felt absolutely amazing, now.

They arrived in Hope to great fanfare. People cheered and tossed confetti. There was dancing in the street, and Smiley gleefully handed out tankards of ale and finger sandwiches.

Rob made an excuse and stepped away, heading up to the castle.

Inside, he found Quinn sitting at his table. But, to Rob's surprise, the man wasn't drinking. In fact, no bottles were on the table, nor were there casks of ale nearby.

Quinn looked up from a parchment he'd been writing on. "Oh, it's you."

"Overlord," Rob said with a bow, then walked past and down the stairs to the lower level. All the while, he felt Quinn's eyes tracking him.

Rob knew the man was up to something, but had no clue what. He still needed to find out.

He crossed the room to the Kingdom Cornerstone, took off a glove and placed his hand on it.

The familiar confirmation message appeared. Skipping the preamble, he went right to the end.

Raise your Kingdom to level Seven?

Yes.

Finished, he stood. He'd gotten the kingdom up another level. Whoopy. It was all a dance he was required to perform.

But, now, he had something truly worth pursuing. And even though he didn't quite know what it meant or entailed, yet, it was going to get done so he could escape this place.

He was going to complete the Great Circle.

Rob's journey continues in the next installment:

Kingdom Level Seven

Also by Adam Drake

An Infinite Cats Mystery
The Big Bag of Infinite Cats: A Cozy Mystery
Magical Mischief: A Cozy Mystery
The River's Dream: A Cozy Mystery
The Model Prisoner

Bitch Berserker
Bitch Berserker: LitRPG Dark Fantasy

Fantasy Double Series
Fantasy Double Series 1

Fantasy & Scifi Double Series
Fantasy & Scifi Double Series 1

Fringe Outlaws
Escape to the Fringe

Kingdom
Kingdom Level One: LitRPG Epic Fantasy
Kingdom Level Two: LitRPG Epic Fantasy
Kingdom Level Three: LitRPG Epic Fantasy
Kingdom Level Four: LitRPG Epic Fantasy
Kingdom Level Five
Kingdom Level Six
Kingdom Level Seven

Kingdom Bundles
Kingdom LitRPG Bundle: Books 1-4
Kingdom LitRPG Bundle: Books 5-7

LitRPG Double Series
LitRPG Double Series 1: Epic Adventure Fantasy
LitRPG Double Series 2: Epic Adventure Fantasy
LitRPG Double Series 3: Epic Adventure Fantasy
LitRPG Double Series 4: Epic Adventure Fantasy

LitRPG: Shadow For Hire
Shadow Gambit: LitRPG Adventure Fantasy
Shadow Hunting: LitRPG Adventure Fantasy
Shadow Wars: LitRPG Adventure Fantasy
Shadow Blade: LitRPG Adventure Fantasy

Mage Level Grind
Mage Level 1
Mage Level 2
Mage Level 3
Mage Level 4
Mage Level 5

SCIFI Double Series
SCIFI Double Series 1: Action Adventure

Total Collapse: Day By Day
The First Day: Post Apocalyptic Thriller

Standalone
Shadow For Hire Books 1-4: LitRPG Adventure Fantasy
The LitRPG Super Bundle: Epic Adventure Fantasy
LitRPG: 5 Books: Epic Adventure Fantasy
SCIFI Double Novel: Science Fiction Adventure
Fantasy Collection: 6 Novels
Science Fiction Collection: 6 Novels
Scifi & Fantasy Megabundle: 12 Novels
Infinite Cats Mysteries: Books 1-3
Mage Levels 1-5

www.ingramcontent.com/pod-product-compliance
Lightning Source LLC
Chambersburg PA
CBHW071323140726

47996CB00005B/1802